HER GARGOYLE PROTECTOR

BEASTLY FALLS

SABRINA SILVERS

ABOUT HER GARGOYLE PROTECTOR

When Amber Lawson flees her abusive ex-boyfriend, she discovers the mysterious town of Beastly Falls—a place where humans and supernatural beings coexist, bound by a curse that only allows fated mates to enter.

Welcomed by the quirky towns people, all eager to get to know her and oddly curious about her relationship status, she quickly finds a job as the night-time librarian. Charmed by the gothic structure and the eclectic collection of books and patrons, she quickly falls into a routine and is intrigued by one of her patrons, a male who resembles the gargoyle on the building.

Gargoyle Xavier Chauvre watches over the library by day and transforms into a brooding human by night, cursed until he finds his true love. He had despaired of ever finding his love until he felt the unmistakable tug the day Amber drove into town. Drawn to her, he lurks in the stacks and keeps watch over her, hoping she feels the bond too.

As sparks fly over late-night book talks, Amber falls into old habits, and only a magical mating bond with Xavier can save her. Can this odd couple break the curse, defeat her past, and find love among the stacks?

BEASTLY FALLS SERIES

In the enchanting town of Beastly Falls, time stands still, and love is put to the ultimate test. Two decades ago, a tragic love story between a human and a monster led the town to trap all its residents within its mystical borders. No one enters, no one leaves—until now. When a human stumbles across the border, everyone is shocked. Then a mate bond appears. Could the curse be finally broken?

If you loved Her Gargoyle Protector, please check out the other books in this fun, small town paranormal romance collaboration: Beastly Falls.

CHAPTER I

AMBER

I drove down the winding forest road and glanced in my rearview mirror, wiping away tears for what felt like the millionth time today. My hands were shaking on the steering wheel, and my stomach growled loud enough to drown out the static-filled radio. The road was empty behind me, and I breathed a sigh of relief. Maybe I had finally ditched Kevin. When he had found me in that last town, I barely escaped before he caught me. I ducked out before the sun was even up to avoid him following me. But now I was running on fumes, needing caffeine and food and a new sanctuary.

I checked the map I had bought. Yes, it was a paper map. I didn't know they still made those. But it was a good thing because my GPS had started going haywire a few miles back. In fact, it showed nothing but green and a large body of water. Yet, it was clearly wrong because I was looking at a quaint sign that read "Welcome to Beastly Falls, Population???" in swirling golden script. Cute name.

The only problem was, it wasn't supposed to be here.

The GPS and the paper map agreed. There was no town

supposed to be here, named Beastly Falls or not. This was an empty stretch of road for at least another hour. Yet there was a town. It may not be on my map, but at this point, I'd take any port in a storm. I hoped they had coffee strong enough to wake the dead, because that's exactly how I felt.

As I pulled into what looked like the main street, lined with the most adorable shops I had ever seen. It looked like a vintage New England town from postcards or the movies. I didn't think they existed. This was so far from my life in Baltimore, but I loved it already. I wondered if I could stay for a while. My eyes landed on a cozy little café called The Growling Bean. Charming. And hopefully not too on-the-nose about their coffee quality.

I parked my beat-up Corolla, grabbed my purse, and stepped out onto the sidewalk. That's when things got weird. Well, weirder.

Every single person on the street froze. And when I say froze, I mean like someone hit the pause button on a movie. But that wasn't even the strangest part. These weren't... people. At least, not entirely.

To my left stood a massive green creature that had more muscles than any body builder that I had ever seen and tusks coming out of his lower jaw. He wore a pinstriped, gray suit with a maroon tie and white dress shirt and was mid-bite into what looked like a gooey cinnamon bun. Beside him, there was a woman dressed in a green and brown homespun dress, with what looked like leaves and branches coming off of it, coming off of her, almost like she was part tree. It was very confusing. And they were staring at me. Because they weren't people. Weren't human. They were monsters.

I rubbed my eyes. Maybe I was more tired than I thought.

"Um, hi?" I managed weakly.

Silence. More staring.

Right. Okay. I remembered vaguely hearing about towns, usually outside of the big cities, that were populated with monsters, or supernaturals as they preferred to be called, since they were more comfortable living among their own kind. Monsters had been living among us for years, but we hadn't ever really known about them until a few decades ago. To say it had not gone well was an understatement, but most people handled it pretty well, though we only saw the occasional supernatural in the city, usually the more common ones, who looked like humans.

It was weird to be the one they would stare at, but I suppose it made sense, since I was probably the minority here, since I didn't see any humans on the street. This was fine. Totally normal. I could handle this. Besides, true monsters didn't always look that way on the outside. I knew that better than anyone. I'd just get my coffee and be on my way to wherever I was going next. Not that I had a clue where that would be.

I pushed open the café door, a little bell announcing my arrival. The low hum of conversation stopped dead inside and all eyes turned to me. The barista—who appeared to be part goat—dropped the mug he was holding, the ceramic shattering on the tile floor. I swallowed and made my way to the counter.

"Can I get a large coffee, please? Cream and sugar." I tried to sound normal, like I ordered from mythical creatures every day.

Before the goat-man could respond, the door burst open behind me. A short, plump woman with rosy cheeks and a head full of curls that defied gravity bustled in, pushing through the crowd of beings who had blocked the door, all staring at me. She maneuvered her way to my side and glared at everyone with exasperation.

"Oh, for heaven's sake, you lot! Have none of you ever seen a human before?" She turned to me with a warm smile, trying to appear grandmotherly. "I apologize, dear. We don't get many visitors here in Beastly Falls. I'm Sylvia Haasenfrau, the mayor."

I shook her offered hand, feeling like I'd stumbled into some bizarre dream. "Amber Lawson. Nice to meet you."

Sylvia shooed away the gawking crowd. "We're so happy to see you. You look so tired, dear. A coffee should fix you up in no time, along with something to eat. Wyn, has she ordered yet?"

I felt a bit like a pine tree buffeted by a windstorm. Sylvia was a force of nature, but the man behind the counter, Wyn, busied himself making my coffee, so I was grateful for the intervention. "Something to eat, dear?"

I scanned the menu on the board, almost too tired to read it. Since it was lunchtime, I settled for soup and half a sandwich, which I relayed. Wyn nodded, acknowledging my order, and handed over the mug of steaming coffee. It smelled like heaven. I dug for my money, but he shook his head. "On the house, miss."

"Thank you."

He smiled, a bit shyly. "Welcome to Beastly Falls."

Sylvia nodded approvingly and steered me towards a two-seat table by the window, glaring over my shoulder at the crowd, who dispersed with mumbles. We settled at the small wrought-iron table and I sipped my coffee. Oh, it was like tasting heaven. Or maybe I was exhausted. Either way, I was immensely grateful for the hit of caffeine flooding my veins.

Sylvia waited a few minutes, studying me, then she spoke. "So, how did you find our little town, Amber?"

"I drove here," I replied, gesturing out front to my car, confused by the question. Maybe I needed more caffeine, or she needed something. What a weird question.

"Hmm," Sylvia said, tapping her chin. "Forgive me for saying, but you look tuckered out, like you could use a good rest. Have you considered staying a while?"

I blinked. "I hadn't really thought about it. But this is a cute town."

Actually, I was tired of moving and had no actual destination in mind. This would be the last kind of town Kevin would ever come to, so it would be the perfect place to settle, at least for a while. And my bank account could use some funding, since I'd been draining it quickly, being on the run for the past few months. I wondered if they would have any job openings? I wasn't picky. It would be too much to ask for that they'd have a librarian position. I'd waitressed in college and worked retail too. I was no stranger to hard work.

Sylvia nodded sagely, folding her hands in front of her. "I can sense these things about people. Did you move recently?"

"You could say that," I mumbled, not wanting to get into the whole fleeing-my-abusive-ex story. It had always been my experience that most people didn't like when you got too personal right away. And when you add in an abusive ex, well, most people found themselves with a pressing appointment or something else to do really fast. No one wanted that kind of trouble. Not that I blamed them. I wish I could avoid this trouble too.

Sylvia, on the other hand, laid a comforting hand on my arm and relief flooded through me, easing my stress. I could feel my muscles relaxing in my shoulders and the tension bleeding out of me. I think my shoulders even lowered from the vicinity of my ears, something they hadn't done in weeks. I could breathe for the first time in so long without the band around my chest. There was something about her that made me wonder who or what she was. While she looked human, I didn't think she was.

Her eyes were kind as she looked at me and I got the sense she knew what was going on. "You don't need to keep running, dear. You're safe here for as long as you stay with us. You seem like you could use a break. We have a lovely bed-and-breakfast owned by Esme Red, just down the street, with a room for rent that might suit you just fine."

I was feeling a bit bewildered, but maybe that was the stress, lack of sleep, and hunger talking. Maybe I had driven into an alternate reality, but I was feeling better, almost like I truly was safe, like Kevin couldn't get to me here and I could take a chance at staying for a while. I needed to replenish my savings, anyway. "That would be great."

Wyn brought my soup and sandwich, along with a salad for Sylvia, and we ate quietly. All the while, I felt like a sideshow attraction with large numbers of onlookers coming into the cafe or walking by and staring at me, deliberately ignoring Mayor Sylvia's pointed glare or even more obvious comments for them to move along. As strange as it all was, it also comforted me. If they reacted to me, a stranger, like this, Kevin could never sneak into Beastly Falls. I would have some warning and be able to escape if he did.

Once I finished eating, I scanned the street, looking at the quaint facades of the shops all along the street. They were all a bit distorted, as if seen through a mirror, by defying the laws of nature. But the brick and stone structures, and canopies were so lovely, I couldn't wait to explore, and hopefully find a job.

I felt a tug towards a stone building in the distance, a beautiful gothic structure a couple of streets away. It was a couple of stories taller than some of the other buildings, standing separately from all other structures, and it had a lone figure standing on the roof.

"What is that building?"

Sylvia followed my gaze. "That's our library. It's open twenty-four hours because we have a lot of nocturnal residents, though we haven't had a nighttime librarian for a while, so there are times when it's closed at night. Do you like to read?"

A library? A town that needs a librarian? It was almost too good to be true. "Something like that," I replied. "Would you be able to direct me to the bed-and-breakfast? I'd love to see if I could get a room."

Sylvia beamed. "Of course. You must be exhausted. I'll take you there now."

We cleared our table, and she ushered me out of the café, chattering about the town's history. As we walked and she pointed out landmarks, I wondered just what I'd gotten myself into. But for the first time in months, I had a glimmer of hope. Maybe, just maybe, Beastly Falls was exactly where I needed to be.

CHAPTER 2
XAVIER

Sunlight heated my stone shell, though I didn't feel it. I never felt it. I spent my days perched atop the library's weathered roof, my granite form an eternal sentinel over the Beastly Falls Library only to emerge in the evening, when my curse lifted, allowing me the freedom to roam the town and speak to my fellow townspeople. I missed the sun, but that was my curse, to be stone until my fated mate set me free. Only, my mate was not in Beastly Falls and, since no one new could come into town or leave, I was doomed to be alone.

My curse was gaining strength, a foothold on my consciousness, taking more time from me, more of my waking time. I struggled to rise to wakefulness in the evenings and I feared the day when I would not waken and would remain a statue, a decoration on this library, forgotten by everyone as someone who once existed.

Most days, I sleep. It's easier that way, to let conscious-ness slip away like water through cupped hands. But today, something stirred me from my stony sleep. A tug to my very soul prodded me to wakefulness, though I could only rise so far. What could it be? There is only one other gargoyle in the town, Asa Graywing, who has been the town protector for several years. We may both be gargoyles, but the curse has affected us differently. We are both driven by our protective natures, driven by our duties, and have shared some of our curses. Asa recently mated with a newcomer to our town. I wonder if he felt this tug, this awareness when his mate came to town?

Hope flared inside of me, white hot and exciting, but like a flame, I worry it will burn me. If my mate is new to town, the curse brought her here. I know from Asa and my friend Rook's recent mating, their females were brought to town and trapped here by the curse, unable to leave until the curse had run its course. Fortunately, they accepted their mates and loved their partners, but that was not a foregone conclusion. And the consequences could be devastating.

When the curse took the town two decades ago, my mother was devastated. She couldn't handle been torn from her family and the outside world. She grew to resent my father, her mate, and her son. I watched her grow bitter and angry as the years passed until she finally died. My father passed soon after, unable to bear being in this world without his mate, despite the relief of no longer being a target for her hatred and vitriol.

I vowed never to force another female to suffer under the curse, even if I was doomed myself. But now, I feared my mate was here and I would have to confront my fears. Would she accept me and the curse, or would she reject me and doom me to stone forever?

I both longed for and dreaded nightfall. But I needed

the answers. Who was my mate? Could I take the chance and pursue her, knowing the risks I took? Dare I doom her to life in Beastly Falls with no escape?

CHAPTER 3
AMBER

Once I rented a room from a lovely woman, Esme Red, who apparently was a werewolf though I couldn't see it, I explored the town, with a focus on finding a job. I wandered down the quaint cobblestone street, trying not to gawk at the colorful assortment of... citizens? Monsters? Fairy tale creatures? I wasn't sure what to call them, but I was definitely not in Kansas anymore. I could see myself living here, at least until Kevin tracked me down and forced me to run again.

I smirked at the idea of Kevin in Beastly Falls. He would hate this town. He had been furious at the open living of monsters in Baltimore, not that there were many living there. We had an orc living down the hall from us and Kevin made nasty comments under his breath whenever he encountered him. Though he was careful to do it once we were out of hearing, since the orc could break Kevin in two without breaking a sweat. If he had dealt with Kevin, I wouldn't have had to leave my life, but my ex had a strong sense of self-preservation, like most cockroaches.

So, maybe I was safe here, at least for a while.

After a few twists and turns, I found myself in front of the library. My jaw dropped. The library was a breathtaking gothic structure, all soaring spires and intricate stonework. It looked like it had been plucked straight out of a Victorian novel and dropped into this quirky little town. I hoped they would let me work here. It was a dream come true to work in a place like this. My last library was a brick box with all the personality of a... well, a brick. But this building seemed laden with secrets and charm. I couldn't wait to explore.

"It's beautiful," I breathed, craning my neck to take it all in.

That's when I spotted him. Perched right in the middle of the roof was a single, imposing gargoyle. His wings were partially unfurled, powerful arms braced against the ledge, and his face... well, now I understood what some people meant when they said a man had a jaw chiseled from granite. This male was literally carved from stone and was stunning. His entire body was a masterpiece that could have been created by the master sculptors of the Renaissance. And his face was a beautiful sight to behold, with sharp, strong features, imposing and confident.

I cleared my throat when I realized I had been gawking at a statue, not even a real, flesh and blood person. Ridiculous.

"I've never seen a building with just one gargoyle before," I mused aloud. "Usually, they come in clans and are not solitary."

"That's usually true, but we only need the one for our building. Our town is very safe, for the most part. Xavier acts as a protector for the library and enforces the library rules. Though there is another gargoyle in town." A voice spoke from next to me, a hint of amusement in her tone.

I jumped and turned to face a middle-aged woman, about my height, with blonde hair. She looked human, like me, but I could swear her eyes shifted for a moment, looking almost cat-like in appearance. But I must have been mistaken. She coolly studied me from head to foot, though I wasn't sure if I was friend or foe. So, I defaulted to making a joke to break the ice.

I chuckled nervously. "Does he swoop down and terrorize people who don't return their books on time? Chase after library patrons with overdue fees?"

To my surprise, the other woman didn't laugh. She only arched an eyebrow. "We rarely have an issue with late fees or unreturned books, thanks to Xavier."

"Right," I said slowly, making a mental note to always return my books on time. Very on time.

After another moment, the woman extended a hand. "I'm Anya Kanea. You must be our newest resident."

"Wow, word certainly gets around," I said, shaking her hand, feeling the prick of nails on my palm.

"You know small towns," Anya said. "Are you looking for something to read during your stay?"

Despite her cool tone, I took the plunge. "Not exactly. I'm hoping to apply for a position. I'm a librarian."

This time, I was sure I saw her eyes change. A faint smile curved her lips. "Well, you'd better come inside and we'll get better acquainted then."

As we approached the heavy wooden doors, I couldn't shake the feeling of being watched. I glanced up one last time at the gargoyle statue. For a split second, I could have sworn those stone eyes were following me. A shiver ran down my spine.

"Everything all right, dear?" Anya asked, her speculative gaze following mine to the middle of the roof.

I shook off the weird feeling. "Oh, yeah. Just admiring the, uh, architecture."

But as the doors closed behind us, I wondered what other surprises this strange little town had in store for me. And why did I have the strangest urge to check out the roof?

~

First day on the job, and I was already neck-deep in... well, literal paperwork. My last job was slightly more advanced than the Beastly Falls library. As in, we had joined the twentieth, and even twenty-first century. But Beastly Falls didn't have any modern equipment. You wanted to check out a book? I dialed the date on a manual handstamp and used an ink pad. You wanted to look for a book from another library? Out of luck. And internet? It was like they had never heard of it. I couldn't even use my cell phone since the service didn't work here.

Anya Kanea, the library director, was giving me the grand tour. She was a no-nonsense kind of woman, with her golden hair pulled back so tightly I wondered if her severe bun was holding her face in place. And she used a lot of cat puns, making me wonder if she had cats at home, but I wasn't going to ask. Honestly, she kind of intimidated me, but I'd dealt with far worse in my time. I wondered if she was human like me, but, since I had yet to see another human, I doubted she was, especially when her eyes had this weird little feline quality to them. Sylvia also might look human, but I wasn't convinced she was. I should use the library resources to do some research on the town and its inhabitants.

"And this is our card catalog," Anya said, gesturing to a massive wooden cabinet with tiny drawers.

I blinked. I guess they really were in the dark ages. "Card catalog? As in, not a computer?"

Anya's lips pursed. "We like to do things the old-fashioned way here. It gives our patrons the purr-sonal touch."

Right. Because nothing said "old-fashioned" quite like a town full of mythical creatures.

"Evelyn Hart will be in for her shift in the morning to relieve you. You can get started on reviewing some of our policies and procedures but, we have a seven day probationary period. I hope you understand," Anya explained, as she handed me two three-inch binders full of paper.

A probationary period? Well, I supposed all jobs had a trial period for new hires. Seven days seemed awfully short, but it would give me some space to figure out if this is where I wanted to stay.

"That would be fine, thank you," I replied.

"And you get two days off during the week. We're open seven days a week, so I'll update the schedule tomorrow. Is that acceptable?"

By her tone, I assumed I should just fall in line. It was fine with me, since I had nothing else to do or anywhere else to be, so I settled for a nod. With that, she swept out of the library, leaving me with the binders and lots of questions about the quirky little town.

As Anya left for the night, I settled in behind the desk, ready for my first shift as the Beastly Falls' night librarian. Technically, the Dewey Decimal System still applied even here, something not affected by time, space or lack of technology. Of course, the library was significantly bigger on the inside than the outside, and it shifted constantly with sections moving around, stacks shifting, and apparently all

I had to do was ask the library what I was looking for and the library would deliver the section to me.

Looking at the names for the sections, I wasn't convinced, knowing the Dewey Decimal System wouldn't help me that much. Arcane Studies. Metaphysical topics. Alchemical Research. I didn't even think those were topics in any categorical system I knew. But one topic did interest me. Town History. Oh yes, please. I loved reading about history, and I sensed Beastly Falls had some very interesting stories in its past.

I lost myself in how the town was founded and kept secret during the centuries when monsters were hidden from the greater world, though they had links to other communities. Slowly the town came into the modern world, creating ties with the human world as monsters exposed themselves and Beastly Falls was on the map.

I closed the narrow tome and stared at the painting of the library's founder across from the circulation desk, a minotaur who apparently hoarded knowledge like a dragon hoards treasure. So Beastly Falls was once public, and people knew about it. So why wasn't it on my map or my GPS? Was it related to why everyone seemed stuck in the past, like using a card catalog and not a computer? And why my cell phone wasn't working?

There had to be something I was missing. It was a small book, almost a cliff notes version, so there had to be more. But I wasn't being paid to read about town history. I had a job to do and I would have to do more research later. For now, I settled in to review the binder of policies and procedures that Anya left for me.

I was consumed with the pages when the solid walnut doors swung open to reveal a woman who looked like she'd just stepped off the cover of "Vampire Vogue"—if that was a thing. With flowing red hair, creamy white skin, and eyes so green they had to be supernatural, she sashayed up to the desk. She smiled, flashing a hint of fang, confirming my suspicions that she was a vampire, though she didn't sparkle like popular movies claimed, nor did she wear black evening wear. She was dressed in skin-tight, deep blue jeans, and a silk green blouse, cut low enough to give more than a hint of cleavage. She was beautiful, and I was super envious of her.

"Well, well," she purred, as her gaze roved over me, "what do we have here? A new face in our little town."

I gulped, hoping my blood didn't smell sweet to her. "Uh, hi. I'm Amber, the new night librarian. Can I help you find something?"

She leaned in, and I swear the temperature rose ten degrees. "I'm Helena Deveraux. And I'm always looking for new... experiences."

Was she flirting with me or sizing me up for lunch? With vampires, it was probably both.

"How about a book recommendation?" I squeaked, not ready for handling vampires on the prowl.

Her perfectly shaped eyebrow rose, amusement still coloring her expression. "If that's all you're offering. What would you recommend, little librarian?"

I seized on the first author that came to mind that I had seen on the library shelves. Some of the more recent authors that I might have recommended were not in the catalog, which surprised me, along with the growing list of things that were making me wonder if I had gone through a time machine when I entered Beastly Falls. "Have you tried Terry Pratchett? Funny, smart, lots of supernatural elements."

I held my breath but, to my surprise, her icy demeanor

thawed slightly, shifting from humor to speculation, though she wasn't quite sold yet. "Pratchett? I'm not familiar. Intriguing."

As I helped Helena find a Discworld novel, the door opened again. This time, a man entered—tall, built like a Greek statue, and I meant that literally, with skin that had an odd grayish tint and wings tucked against his back. I did a double take. Yes, there were wings on his back, not feathered ones but dark gray leathery wings. He wore a black t-shirt molded to a body that seemed carved from granite, each muscle clearly defined under his dark gray, rough skin. His hair was jet black, shoulder length, and curled slightly at the ends, looking silky smooth, the only soft part of him. Even his eyes were hard, deep black, and intense when he stared at me. He looked strangely familiar, though I couldn't place why.

Our eyes met, and I felt a jolt of something. Recognition? Déjà vu? I didn't know how to explain it but I felt almost like I knew him, like something bound us together.

He froze, our eyes meeting, then he made his way to the reading area, and I felt oddly disappointed. I had hoped he would come to the desk, speak to me, acknowledge this strange connection between us. Yet, he turned away as if he didn't feel it. I didn't even know him, but I felt oddly disappointed. I turned my attention back to Helena and explained the series to her despite her clear suspicions, but a part of me was aware of the male across the room. He picked up a book, but I noticed his gaze never left me.

Great. My first night on the job, and I already had a vampire who either wanted to be my friend or have me for lunch and a potential stalker. I thought I had left that issue behind me.

I sighed, reaching for the stamp to check out Helena's

book. "Welcome to Beastly Falls," I muttered to myself. "Where the patrons are stranger than fiction, and the librarian might be losing her mind."

Helena gave me a sharp look but glided out of the library. At least the gargoyle hadn't come to life and started collecting overdue fees. Yet. Though, there was something about that male...

CHAPTER 4
XAVIER

Once night completely fell, my body slowly reanimated. I stretched carefully, feeling the stone that encapsulated my muscles and bone dissipate and be replaced by flesh. My skin kept the grayish cast that I maintained from the stone during the day, but it was warmer, more supple, if still rough. I worked through the gentle stretching exercises and yoga poses that Evinara from the Twilight Tree yoga studio had taught me several years ago when I mentioned struggling with the transition from stone to flesh. As the years went on without finding a mate, the shift between forms was harder and longer, and I wondered how much longer I had before I was frozen on the top of the library.

The tug in my chest intensified, and I stretched my wings out, letting them gently lower me to the ground, instead of taking the long way down, via the interior back stairs. I scanned Main Street, the darkened storefronts, noting the ones that remained open for the nocturnal inhabitants. I searched inside myself for the thread that had anchored itself inside of me and turned back to the library,

23

my home for many long years. She was there. Inside. My possible mate. I scarcely dared to hope. After all these long years, could it be?

Instead of heading into town for dinner, I was drawn into the library. Not unusual since I was its guardian, but food held little appeal when I suspected my mate was inside. I opened the huge, solid wood double doors and let my eyes adjust to the bright lights. My eyes, my entire being, focused on the new human in town, one of the very few who remained after the curse.

Someone else might have found her unremarkable, but she was beautiful to my eyes. Her red hair was long and thick and pulled back at the nape of her neck. She was tall, but not at tall as I was, curvy in all the right places, her breasts the perfect handful for me. Her hips were gently rounded, and I could imagine holding them as I pounded into her from behind or between her thighs.

She could easily handle a gargoyle and my strength, not someone with whom I would need to be careful, which was good for me, because when the mating frenzy came over me, I might not be as careful as I should be. Her hazel eyes settled on me and awareness flared in them. Her mouth opened slightly, then her attention was pulled away by Helena Deveraux, the vampire who always pushed the limits of everyone she came across, testing them. I debated stepping in, but wasn't ready to expose who the female might be to me, especially to Helena, who was far too perceptive.

I grabbed a book from the spotlight section, not that we've added any new books in years, and sat in the reading area, the book in my hands nothing more than a prop. I had read almost every book in the library, some more than once, but I wasn't here to read. I was completely focused on her—

Amber, the new librarian, as I overheard Helena call her. She moved like a dancer. Her smile was a beacon of warmth in this cold existence I'd endured for so long. She greeted patrons and spoke kindly to everyone.

The pull towards her was undeniable, unlike anything I'd felt in my centuries of life. Could it truly be a mating bond? The very thought sent a thrill of hope through me, quickly followed by a wave of fear. Hope was dangerous here in Beastly Falls. Hope could break you.

I watched sharply as she interacted with Helena. Helena was accustomed to being the center of attention wherever she went. Yet she too was feeling the pinch of loneliness, having not found her mate among the residents of the town. She easily found companionship and blood donors as needed, but nothing replaced the bond of a mate, the close ties, the connection we all longed for. Yet, even faced with Helena's intimidating presence, Amber held her ground, offering book recommendations with genuine enthusiasm, not realizing that most of us were tired of the same old books and were unfamiliar with the titles or authors she spoke of, since nothing new had come into our town since the curse took effect.

Amber's gentleness called to something deep within me. But I remain rooted to my chair, unable to approach. Fear held me back. The curse had taken so much from us already. If I was wrong about this feeling, if she rejected me, I wasn't sure I could bear it.

The chair beside me scraped against the floor as Rook Mullein, a vampire and my closest friend, sat down. His eyes followed my gaze to Amber.

"So," he said quietly, "that's her, isn't it? The one you sensed entering town?"

I nodded, not trusting my voice.

Rook leaned back, his expression thoughtful. "You think it might be a mating bond?"

"I don't know," I admitted, the words heavy with frustration and longing. "It feels different. Powerful. But after all this time, how can I be sure?"

"The curse has been weakening," Rook mused. "It happened to me only a couple of weeks ago, when I met my Jenny. Maybe it's your turn."

I shifted in my seat to face him, the lumpy chair groaning under my weight, seeing my own conflicted emotions mirrored in his eyes. "And if it's not? If I'm just grasping at false hope?"

Rook sighed, running a hand through his perfectly coiffed hair. "Then you go on as you have been. But Xavier, at some point, you have to take the risk. If there's even a chance of breaking this curse, of finding your mate, trust me, it's worth it."

"The fall will be that much harder if I'm wrong," I countered.

Rook had found his mate, in the edgy and bright Jenny Cortado, when her car had broken down in town a few weeks ago. She had not been able to leave once she entered the town. And when the mating bond had initiated, she could have doomed my friend to a half-life and eventual death if she had rejected the bond. But she hadn't. She accepted the bond and him. It saved him, broken his curse. And because of it, he could walk during the day and sustain himself on only Jenny's blood. I had watched him suffer, agonizing if she could accept him. Could I take the same risk?

We sat in silence for a moment, watching as Amber cheerfully helped another patron. Her laughter carried across the library, and it resonated in my chest.

"She's human," I mumbled. "Even if the bond is real, how could she ever accept someone like me? A monster who turns to stone by day? And will she even want to stay?"

Rook placed a hand on my shoulder. "You're not a monster, Xavier. And if she's truly your mate, she'll see that too. But you'll never know if you don't take that first step. She could be your salvation, breaking your curse."

I nodded, knowing he's right but still hesitating. The weight of centuries of loneliness and the fear of rejection warred within me.

As if sensing my gaze, Amber looked up, her eyes meeting mine across the room. For a moment, just a heartbeat, something flickered in her expression, maybe even a hint of the same longing I feel.

"Go talk to her," Rook urged gently.

I sucked in a deep breath, steeling myself. "Tomorrow," I promised, both to Rook and myself. "I'll approach her tomorrow."

Rook eyed me reproachfully and opened his book. Feeling the weight of his expectation, like so many others in town hoping for their mate, I turned back to Amber. And I allowed myself to hope, just a little, that maybe—just maybe—our curse is finally nearing its end.

Heart pounding, I rose from my seat, intending to exit quietly. But my departure was interrupted by the library door flinging open. A disheveled male stumbled in, his eyes wild and unfocused. I narrowed my gaze at him and realized he was one of the troll brothers from the bridge. They were not known for being the most intelligent of beings, but they rarely strayed from their bridge and were generally amiable, though they could be stubborn. When he focused on Amber, I sensed there was about to be trouble.

He advanced on the circulation desk where Amber was standing, her eyes wide and uncertain. The troll, I wasn't sure which brother it was since they looked alike, planted his hands on the desk. "I'm Jabir. My brothers and I need a mate. You be our mate?"

Amber stepped back, the scent of fear growing. Without thinking, I slid between them, spreading my wings to shield Amber, pushing Jabir back, creating a barrier between her and the troll. "She is not for you or your brothers, Jabir," I said firmly, my voice low and menacing. My wings widened further, the claws on the tips extending, ready if he attempted to force his way through me. An urge to rend him limb from limb if he touched her possessed me, a desire to protect Amber at all costs, riding me hard.

Jabir blinked, seeming to consider his next thoughts, as if sensing my rage. But he set his jaw. "We need a mate. She is new to town. Must be a mate."

Trolls might be thick-headed, but they certainly weren't stupid. I understood his desire for a mate, the desperation that rode him. It drove me, too. So, I throttled back my anger and repeated my words. "She is not your mate, Jabir." I leveled a hard stare at him, folding my arms in front of me and letting my wings flare out to their full extent, hiding Amber and the desk from his view, hopefully discouraging him.

He considered me as a potential adversary for a mate. I saw his consideration in his eyes, wondering if he could take me on and win. A part of me hoped he wouldn't create more of a scene than he already had, but the inner beast in me wanted to show off for my mate. Finally, he muttered a half-assed apology and retreated hastily, leaving the library with a bang of the door.

I turned to Amber, her fear still scenting the air, worried I'd frightened her further. While fear still lurked there, I also saw gratitude.

"Thank you for your help," she said softly. "I'm still adjusting to the town. He was scary."

I nodded, not trusting myself to speak. A powerful urge to pull her close, to protect her from all harm, that almost swamped me, but I couldn't risk it. Not yet.

"He was just hoping you were his mate. Next time, just be firm and tell him to back off."

Her eyes widened. "Next time?"

I didn't have the heart to tell her that this might be a regular occurrence until everyone found out she was my mate. The mating bond urged me to mark her so everyone knew she was mine, but I knew it was too soon. She still had remnants of fear in her eyes. Whether it was from Jabir or something else, I wasn't sure. But I sensed I had to tread lightly. Only, I didn't have much time to ease her into the reality of our connection.

"Don't worry. Almost everyone will be a bit more kind in their approach," I reassured her, even as I vowed to do my best to watch out for her. When I could, that is.

"Thanks. That's good to know." She hesitated, her hand on a stack of books. "I should probably get back to work."

I knew I should walk away, avoid any disappointment, but with Rook's encouragement echoing in my mind, I remained standing at the desk, where Amber sorted through a stack of returned books.

"Maybe you can help me," I said, my voice rougher than intended as I stepped closer.

Amber lifted her head, her eyes widening as she realized

I had moved closer, my size making me almost loom over her. For a moment, fear flashed across her face again, and anger burned within me. Who put that fear there? Who dared to hurt her? A surge of protective rage coursed through my veins, and I consciously had to relax my clenched fists, lower my raised wings that had extended in preparation for a battle.

"I'm sorry," I made my voice soften, though it was difficult, and I took a deliberate step back. "I didn't mean to frighten you. I'm Xavier."

Tension eased from her shoulders, though wariness still lingered in her eyes. "Amber," she replied, a tentative smile on her face. "Is there something I can help you find?"

I leaned in slightly, unable to help myself, trying to catch a whiff of her scent. "Who made you afraid?" The words slipped out before I could stop them.

Amber stiffened again, her smile forced, though alarm flashed through her eyes. "I'm not sure what you mean. Now, about that book?"

I recognized the deflection for what it was and reluctantly let it go. For now. "Actually, I was hoping you could recommend a book for me to read. I've heard you have quite the passion for books. It would be a pleasure to talk books with someone new."

Her face lit up, and the sight stole my breath away. "Oh! Well, in that case, what's your favorite genre?"

"I prefer the classics, but am open to all kinds of literature." I didn't want to tell her that I had read just about everything in the library over the past couple of decades, except for certain genres. "What's your favorite book?"

She blushed faintly, the color highlighting her cheeks. "I love to read romance, but I didn't see a lot of them on the shelves, at least not the more recent titles. But, I also love the classics. I read Pride and Prejudice every year."

I didn't want to insult Amber's taste in books, but romance was the one area I hadn't read. I had avoided the genre, not wanting to even consider romance in my future, though I had never been drawn to reading them. I preferred the works of Homer, Chaucer, Milton, but I felt that might be too pretentious, as Rook often accused me of being. But the passion that Amber began speaking of her favorite books was infectious, and I wondered if I should broaden my horizons.

Suddenly, I realized she'd stopped speaking and was looking at me expectantly. "I haven't read them," I was forced to admit.

Disappointment shadowed her expression. "I understand. Not many men like romances."

"Maybe you can recommend one for me," I asked, hating the tone of disappointment in her voice.

"If I can find it! Your library is laid out a little differently than I am used to. Pride and Prejudice might be a good one for you," she smiled.

"I can help you find it," I offered.

"Great and maybe you can show me something you like to read."

"Deal."

I lead her to the classical literature section, housed under the Old Tomes of Ancient Times, and handed her my prized possession. A rare first edition of 'Paradise Lost' by John Milton.

"This is incredible," she breathed, handling the slim volume delicately. "I've never seen anything like it. I can't believe you have this here and not in a private collection somewhere more protected."

"Anya is a talented archivist. What about you?" I asked, genuinely curious. "What draws you to the romance genre?"

Amber sighed. "I suppose I love the idea of finding the one person who is perfect for you, but it's more than that. I love the themes of social class and the whole cultural themes they leverage in their books. Maybe that's why I love reading historical romance. The regency era and the social class hierarchy, forbidden love between people who cannot be together but love each other, is catnip to me."

"Don't let Anya hear that or she'll get excited," I teased. Amber cocked her head at me, clearly not understanding me. "Anya is a cat shifter. Catnip means something else to her."

Amber's eyes widened for a moment, then she let out a laugh that was like music to my ears. "I'll remember that."

She reached for a volume on a higher shelf, stretching on tiptoes to get to it, but didn't quite get there. I easily plucked the volume from the top shelf, our hands brushing. The contact sent a jolt through me, and Amber's breath caught. For a moment, we froze, the air between us charged with tension.

She smiled, glanced down, and gestured to the book. "You should read Pride and Prejudice. It's a wonderful story. I envy Elizabeth with her insistence on marrying for love, even though it goes against the culture of the time. She also refuses to accept Darcy's proposal, even though it would help her family financially, and she waits for his declaration of love. She won't accept anything less than his honesty. She's so brave. I wish I could be that brave, sometimes."

The bell dinged at the front desk, and she jolted. "I'm sorry. I should really get back to the desk."

"Of course. I'm sorry I monopolized so much of your time," I replied. "But perhaps we could continue our discussion another time?"

She gave me a brilliant smile this time, and it was like the sun breaking through clouds. "I'd like that."

As I reluctantly turned to leave, I felt that something has shifted. The mating bond, if that's truly what this was, pulsed stronger than ever.

CHAPTER 5
AMBER

I don't know why I thought the night-shift would be quiet. Either Beastly Falls had a surprising number of nocturnal patrons or something else was going on because I was kept hopping at the front desk after I found Xavier his book. Xavier had settled in the easy chair in the front of the library, in a cozy chair that looked made for him, with cutouts for his wings, and began to read. Honestly, I had expected him to be patronizing me, saying he was going to read Pride and Prejudice then set it aside as soon as my back was turned, but every time my gaze strayed towards him, which was often, he appeared engrossed in the story, though he often met my gaze with a wicked grin.

It had been a long time since I had found a male attractive. I hadn't even considered another male, so worried I was about Kevin and how he would react, even after we'd broken up. But I suspected if Kevin somehow showed up in Beastly Falls, Xavier could handle himself just fine. His muscles that seemed carved from granite were clearly defined under the charcoal t-shirt, and the thick thighs that strained the seams of his denim showed that he could hold his own against a bully like my ex easily. Despite his size, easily towering over me, I didn't feel afraid, even when we were in the narrow aisles of the bookshelves. I felt safe, protected. Maybe it was because he saved me from the troll, or maybe because he showed he cared for how I felt. Either way, I sensed Xavier was different, and my gaze kept stealing to him as I checked out patrons and answered their questions as best I could.

Though some questions were a little more challenging. A tall, willowy male with pointed ears glided in at one point, his voice sounding almost musical as he asked me my name. He then invited me to dinner, and I had an irresistible urge to go, while something inside screamed no!

A low rumble from the easy chair and a rustle of wings broke the spell, and the male cast an alarmed glance over. "My apologies," he said, bowing slightly. "I did not understand."

And he left with alacrity. That was weird. But the whole evening was weird, so who was I to judge?

Several more patrons came in with at least two more offers of coffee or tea, if that was more thing. All the requests were quickly retracted after a furtive look at Xavier, who did nothing more than shift in his seat and glare. I may not have wanted to accept the offers, but he wasn't my social director.

I probably should have felt more threatened. Kevin used to do the same, only he would have stood right next to the desk and bullied his way against people, and I would have felt his wrath later.

A shadow fell across the desk and I looked up to see a male in a button-down shirt, khaki pants, and a bouquet of gorgeous flowers. Another admirer. In another time, maybe even before Xavier, I would have been flattered. He had a nicely trimmed stubble, shoulder-length dark hair, gold eyes, and a lean body that, sadly, did nothing for my feminine parts.

"Welcome to Beastly Falls, milady. I wondered if I could escort you to your resting place after your shift?" He gave a slight bow and handed me the flowers.

I smiled, charmed by his formal speech and courtly ways, even if they were out of place in the modern era, though in Beastly Falls, maybe it was commonplace. And yet, I knew I would say no. My attention was drawn elsewhere. Xavier growled, and the male paled, glancing over at Xavier who had closed the book, his eyes flashing red. "I didn't realize you were taken. I apologize for any offense. Good evening."

He gave a low bow to Xavier, his eyes fixed on the ground. I think he would have peed if he stayed longer, then he bolted for the door. This had gone on long enough. I stalked around the circulation desk and over to Xavier. Since he was sitting, I at least felt like I had some measure of power over him.

I poked my finger in his chest. "Listen here, Xavier. You don't get to growl at people for talking to me. You don't get to decide who I talk to. Only I can do that. Understand? If you make that mistake again, we're going to have a problem."

A choked laugh came from the other chair in the corner. The tall vampire male covered his mouth and stood. "I think you have this well in hand, Amber. Good day."

I ignored him and glared at Xavier who had a soft smile on his lips. "I think you have plenty of bravery like your favorite character, Elizabeth Bennet, just as she confronted

Mr. Darcy at the ball. I will endeavor to be more circumspect."

Somewhat satisfied, but thrown off balance that he had read that much of my favorite book, I went back to the desk and sat on my stool. Only after I was seated did I realize I had just yelled at a much stronger male and didn't worry about his reaction or if he would hurt me. Maybe I was becoming brave.

~

My shift ended with no further excitement or requests for dates. I was oddly disappointed, even if I would never accept. Xavier had left a couple of hours previously, saying that he needed to get something to eat, and his friend Rook had returned. I felt like Xavier was handing off guard duty to his friend and, while I didn't want it, I was reassured to have a friendly face in the library. Rook was a pleasant male and had delicious tea that he brought, along with regaling me with tales of his mate, Jenny. I couldn't wait to meet her.

The time came to hand over my duties to the shy older woman from the day shift. Evelyn Hart was a short woman, maybe in her mid-forties, gently rounded in all places, with laugh lines and a kind smile. Her soft brown hair was cut in short curls around her face, and she reminded me of someone I could relax with and not have to be worried about impressing.

We chatted for a few minutes about the evening's patrons and any outstanding requests, then I gathered my things to leave. It felt weird leaving my job in the morning and not locking up. Evelyn eyed me with a knowing smile.

"I heard you had some excitement last night. Beastly Falls has a unique welcoming committee."

I laughed. "They certainly do, though I didn't expect all the requests for dates. It will take some getting used to."

Evelyn laid a comforting hand on my arm, and I swore I felt a soothing energy fill my soul. "You've barely been here a day, dear. It's only natural for you to still be finding your footing. Beastly Falls is a unique town, but a wonderful one, filled with good people who will embrace you as one of their own if you let them."

I sighed. "I can't stay for long. There's too much in my past. I can't risk it."

Evelyn only studied me with wise eyes, as if she knew what, and who, was chasing me. "You might be surprised what can happen when you stop running. Sometimes we need to face our past to have the future we deserve."

I stared at her and resisted the urge to retort that she didn't know the struggle and I was only protecting her and the people of Beastly Falls. Instead, I bid her good night, or good morning, or whatever it was, and headed out the front door, only to see Xavier leaning against the stone pillar by the steps, his arms folded in front of him. For a moment, I thought he was part of the stone, his skin grayish in tone with an almost rough quality to it, but then he pushed off the pillar and straightened, his arms dropping to his side, wings flaring out slightly, then tucking back against his back. I was dying to ask him what species he was, but I sensed that might be rude, so I refrained.

"May I escort you to your lodgings?" he asked, his deep voice and oddly formal words giving me a sensation of fizzy bubbles in my chest.

I nodded wordlessly, unsure why this strong, muscular male, who I should find intimidating, instead made me feel safe and roused all kinds of feelings that I thought had been killed by my ex. Of course, if Xavier hadn't reacted badly when I confronted him, I think I was safe with him. Careful to keep a separation between us, since I was still cautious, we walked through the moonlit streets. Xavier pointed out various shops and introduced me to the nocturnal residents we passed.

I noticed that few of the residents had cell phones or tablets or any modern technology that I was accustomed to. Whereas in Baltimore, everyone was always on their phones, barely looking around or talking to anyone else. It was odd. Though, maybe they had the same issue that I had when my cell phone went haywire, and I couldn't get a signal. Maybe they don't have towers or were in a dead zone. But that seemed unlikely in this modern age.

"Xavier, it feels like I stepped back in time here in Beastly Falls. There are no cell phones, no computers. It's odd, isn't it?"

Granted, it may only have been a couple of decades. It wasn't like we were going back to the 1800s, but it was significant enough. My cell phone didn't work and my GPS went haywire as soon as I drove into town. Working in the library, it was strange not having interlibrary loan or the internet to look up requests or do research for the patrons. And no one seemed to care. They accepted it in stride, even Evelyn and Anya.

He sighed, his expression growing somber. "It's the curse," he explained.

"Curse?" I stumbled over my feet, and Xavier gently caught me from falling. A curse? What was that all about? And what had I gotten myself into?

"Years ago, two young lovers, a human and a monster, from families in town were forbidden to be together. They were driven apart and died because of the feud. No one realized how deeply it affected the town until everything shut down. We can't leave and no one can come in until we prove love is real."

I gasped, my heart aching for him and the town's inhabitants. "That's terrible! How can you prove that?"

"We don't know. It's been about two decades. It doesn't seem that long, but when you're living in it, stuck in limbo, it feels like forever. It's been so long, many have lost hope," Xavier replied, his voice filled with sadness.

We walked in silence as the sky lightened with the sun beginning to rise. Pinks and reds streaked the darkness and Xavier's pace picked up, as if he was running out of time. I stepped up my pace to keep up with his longer legs.

"Do you have somewhere to be?" I teased, wanting to add a quip about the sun turning him to stone or something, wondering if he truly was a gargoyle, as I suspected. I knew from legends that gargoyles were stone during the day and he resembled the one on top of the library, so I was pretty sure my hunch was accurate.

As we stopped in front of Red's Bed and Breakfast, he turned a somber gaze to me. "Something like that. I wish I could have taken you to breakfast, but time runs short for me. Esme will have breakfast ready for you, though. You're safe here, Amber. I'll make sure of it. Save dinner for me?"

Feeling oddly touched by his words, I nodded, tears pricking my eyes. "Thank you, Xavier. I look forward to tonight."

I didn't want to add that it had been so long since I had felt safe, had been among people who were kind to me.

Xavier paused at the door and stroked a finger down my cheek, sending shivers down my spine. "Sleep well," he said softly, his eyes searching mine.

"Thank you. For everything," I replied, suddenly reluctant to say goodnight.

He studied me intently for a long moment, then turned and flew off into the sky towards the library, settling into place on the roof. My hunch was confirmed. He was the gargoyle that had so entranced me when I stood at the entrance to the library. I watched as he slowly shifted position until he faced my direction, not straight towards the front of the library, as was his typical position. He settled into place just as the sun peeked over the horizon, the rays shining behind him.

A warmth spread through my chest at the realization. He wasn't just protecting the library. He was protecting me. For the first time since fleeing my ex, I felt safe. As Xavier's form slowly turned to stone in the growing light, I whispered a quiet "thank you" before heading inside.

CHAPTER 6
AMBER

I woke up feeling more refreshed than I had in months. The deep sleep that had eluded me since fleeing Baltimore and my ex-boyfriend had finally found me in this strange little town. As I stretched, my eyes automatically drifted to the library across the street and the gargoyle statue on the top of the library. Somewhere deep inside, I knew he was the reason for my peaceful rest. Knowing that he watched over me and ensured that I was safe allowed me to rest and feel safe. I gave a little wave, feeling foolish since he was a statue and couldn't see me.

I turned back to my room, shaking my head, chuckling at my imagination. Just a few short months ago, I worked in a library in Baltimore, no monsters in sight, except for the orcs in our building. Now, everywhere I looked, there were monsters, yet they seemed nicer than many of the humans I knew from outside this small town. Also, I dreamt about a gargoyle, imagining him watching over me, keeping me safe from the real monster chasing me. I didn't quite understand how a statue came to life and became the man I had a wonderful conversation with last evening, but I knew deep inside, the gargoyle on the roof was Xavier. I didn't have to understand it. This was Beastly Falls and all sorts of strange things were possible. Maybe I was even safe here.

Thinking about Xavier brought a remembered heat, a slow burn of desire that I hadn't felt in a long time. Xavier may be a statue during the day, stone and forbidding stance, but in the evening, he was all hard muscle and intense eyes, with a sharp mind, someone willing to even read a romance on my recommendation. My cheeks flushed as I remembered the way his shirt had clung to his broad chest, how his strong hands had gestured as he spoke passionately about the books he loved. There was definitely nothing stone-like about the man, except maybe his chiseled jawline.

I shook my head and got ready for work. I had no business thinking about any male, physically gorgeous, remarkably intelligent, or anything. I was only here temporarily until I could figure out my next steps, though a part of me wondered if I could stay for longer, maybe even permanently.

As I headed downstairs, Esme Red, the sweet werewolf owner of the B&B, greeted me with a grandmotherly smile. "Sleep well, dear? I have your dinner ready for you."

"Better than I have in ages. Your rooms are so comfortable. Thank you so much. I didn't expect dinner. I was going to grab something on the way to the library," I said, feeling embarrassed that I had slept so long. I never expected to sleep the day away, but somehow I had slept long past when I thought I would wake up and now it was almost time for my shift and I had no time left to explore the town and pick up any essentials.

She waved her hand in the air as if brushing off my

protests. "Don't worry, dear. You need something to wake you up in the morning. I thought you might need a few things since you were light on your luggage when you checked in. If you have any laundry, you can leave it in the hamper in your bathroom, and I can take care of that for you."

I felt tears prick my eyes at her mothering ways. She saw my glistening eyes and hurried over, enfolding me in her arms. "I didn't mean to make you cry, dear. I'm sorry."

I shook my head, sniffling a little. "You didn't. It's been so long since anyone has done anything nice for me. Most people just go about their business and ignore everything going on."

Like the time Kevin tried to drag me into his car. People walked by, averting their gaze and moving to the other side of the street to avoid us, as if nothing was happening. I only got away because he heard sirens and dropped my arm. Sadly, the sirens had nothing to do with us, but I had escaped.

"Nonsense, dear. You're here in Beastly Falls. We look out for our own here. And now, you're one of us," Esme declared. "Now, sit and eat something. Just a warning. It's a full moon tonight, so things may be a bit more rowdy in town than you're used to."

I wasn't sure I could eat anything, but I obediently sat at the table and dug into a delicious dinner of fluffy pancakes, crispy bacon, and mouthwatering fruit. "More rowdy? Things were pretty active at the library last night."

I didn't want to think about all the offers for dinner and coffee from various males, or how Xavier had stepped in, even from his chair. I wasn't sure I was ready for anything more than that tonight. Esme paused in her cleaning the kitchen, slowly turning an amused look on me.

"I heard you had quite a few patrons last night. Don't worry. It won't be anything like that tonight. Most of the shifters in town will be running in their fur. The witches and magical beings often have ceremonies to perform. Leaving a few for their own worship, as it may be. But some of the fur beings might run loose from the forest and come through town, especially if they sense a newcomer among us. If you see them, stand firm. Don't run. And firmly tell them, no. They'll listen." She paused, her lips quirking in a small smile. "Or stay close to Xavier. He'll handle any issues."

I blushed and refocused on my dinner, unsure how to respond to that. After a moment, I had to ask the question that had been bothering me. "Esme, what can you tell me about the curse?"

Her hands dropped in the dishwater, and she sighed, staring out the kitchen window. "It's a sad thing, Amber. A result of people interfering where they shouldn't. Love is beautiful, and those in love should never be forced to choose."

The pain in her voice hurt my heart. "Did you lose someone?"

She came and sat at the table. "My mate passed away several years ago, after the curse took effect. I had many years with him and we had children. But they have not found their mates. They haven't been able to leave Beastly Falls to find someone, nor has anyone come into town to test the bonds. I had hoped that you... well, that's neither here nor there."

I cocked my head, puzzled by her unfinished thought. "What do you mean, Esme?"

"Only mates can come into town. We have seen a couple of new people come into town and they have only been able to find us because they have a bond with someone here. They must choose to remain with their mate or be banished forever."

Her words caused a chill inside of me. Xavier had not mentioned this part of the curse. "What happens to the mate who remains?"

"If the bond is rejected? No one knows for sure, but we suspect the mate dies."

When I was done, Esme handed me a bag for lunch at the library and pushed me out the door, pointing me in the right direction to ensure I knew where to go. The sun had set and shadows were lengthening along the sidewalk. While I would have been nervous in a city, I felt perfectly safe here in Beastly Falls. I pulled my jacket a little tighter around me against the evening chill and headed down the front path to the sidewalk.

Just as I reached the front gate, I spotted Xavier waiting on the sidewalk, leaning against the large oak tree, his wings flared slightly. My heart did a little flip.

"May I walk you to the library?" Xavier extended his arm like a cavalier gentleman from a bygone era, and I was enchanted. "I haven't finished the book yet, but Elizabeth has just rejected Darcy's proposal. I suppose I understand why she rejected him. He didn't exactly propose for the right reasons."

We dove into a lively discussion about Elizabeth and Darcy, and whether she should have accepted him or not, both of us agreeing that she should have declined, and before I knew it, we were at the library. Strangely, there wasn't a soul in sight.

"It's the full moon," Xavier explained, noticing my confusion. "Many of our residents have ceremonies to attend or are affected by it, like our shifters. It'll be a quiet night."

"Esme mentioned that. I guess I won't have any suitors tonight, so no protection needed," I teased.

As we stepped inside, the heavy doors slammed shut behind us with an ominous thud. A click sounded with a finality that made my heart pound in my throat. I spun around and tugged at the handle, almost frantically. It wouldn't budge. I swallowed against the lump in my throat, trying to calm my breathing and not spiral into a panic attack that I sensed was looming at the thought of being trapped in a building with unknown people.

"Xavier," I said, striving for an even tone, "I think we're locked in."

Xavier narrowed his gaze at me, then frowned at the door. He joined me in the small foyer, his arm brushing mine and sending a shiver down my spine. "That's unusual," he muttered, giving the door an experimental push, then harder as he leaned into heavy wood.

We were standing close together, the warmth radiating from his body in the cool library air. I wrapped my arms around myself, trying to relax, but darkness flirted along the edges of my vision, narrowing my sight. Xavier laid a heavy hand on my lower back, the warmth and weight an immediate grounding for me, comforting me. Despite the bizarre situation, I felt an inexplicable sense of calm at his touch. Maybe being locked in a magical library with a handsome, possible-gargoyle man wasn't the worst thing that could happen.

"Are you all right?" Concern echoed in his tone and I pasted on a bright smile, already feeling more centered with him there.

"Well," I said, attempting to lighten the mood and to

keep the panic from spiraling inside of me, "I guess we'll have plenty of time to discuss more books, huh?"

Xavier studied me for a long moment as if he wasn't sure he believed me, then his serious expression softened into a smile that made my heart skip a beat. "I suppose we will," he agreed, his eyes never leaving mine.

CHAPTER 7
XAVIER

The moment the doors slammed shut, I felt the mating bond pulse deep inside. It had only grown over the day time, not weakened, so any thoughts that the bond might not be true, was eradicated. All day, even in my stone form, I had been acutely aware of Amber's presence in town, the mate bond creating a pull between us that I was constantly aware of. Unable to sink into my usual dormant state, I had remained focused on her, feeling the sun's warmth on my granite body as if I were truly coming to life again. Now it appeared the library itself was conspiring to bring us together, a matchmaker of sorts.

Hope blossomed within me, a dangerous, fragile thing I dared not fully embrace. The fear of rejection still loomed large, but it seemed the library itself was conspiring to give us time to explore this connection.

Yet when I saw the flicker of panic in Amber's eyes at being trapped, my heart sank. Something in her past had clearly left its mark, making her terrified of being confined with a male without an escape route. Every instinct screamed at me to pull her close, to comfort and protect her, but I knew that wasn't what she needed right now.

I contented myself with a calming hand on her, and was pleased to feel her emotions settle through the bond. We may not have been fully linked, not yet, but she was responding to me as if we were mated. I feared the completion of the bond was a mere formality at this point, that she was my mate and there would be no other if she decided to forsake me.

Needing some time with my thoughts, I took a step back, giving her space. "I will continue reading that book you recommended. If you need anything, call my name. I will hear you."

I neglected to mention that I could now feel her through the bond and would respond to any change in her emotions. I sensed she wasn't ready for that. Amber nodded and headed for the desk, sorting through books and the task list Anya had left for her. Once I was satisfied that she was settled, I ventured further into the library to see if Rook had arranged my surprise. Once the area was set up for my specifications, I went searching for my mate.

I found Amber in the stacks, shelving books. "I have a surprise for you. Come with me," I said, holding out my hand.

She hesitated a moment, eyeing me with some suspicion, but none of the panic or stress I sensed earlier. Then she placed her soft hand in mine. I led her to the center of the study area, where I had prepared a picnic earlier with the items Rook had gathered and left for me. Knowing most of the town's inhabitants would be occupied with the full moon, I had hoped to create a moment of peace for us, away from prying eyes, and Rook had been my willing accomplice.

I had spread a red and white checkered tablecloth on the floor, possibly a little trite, but I didn't mind. We had a large wicker picnic basket filled with food from the Growling Bean café—charcuterie, a variety of cheeses and meat and assorted crackers, finger sandwiches I hoped Amber would like, fruit including grapes and strawberries, and wine from one of our vineyards. I also had a tray that doubled as a small table and some pillows for us to sit on, since I knew from experience that the library floor was not the most comfortable.

When she saw the picnic laid out, her face lit up with delight, and the sight sent a wave of satisfaction through me. It soothed my soul, my male half, to see her happy, to know I had provided for her in some small way.

"You did this for me?" she asked, her voice filled with wonder.

I nodded, suddenly feeling almost shy. "I thought you might enjoy a break from the usual routine."

"But what if patrons come in?"

I pointed to the full moon shining through the windows. "I doubt we'll see anyone tonight. They're out enjoying the full moon celebrations. You'll have a calm night. In previous months, during the full moon, we used to close the library to let everyone enjoy the evening. Some of us don't celebrate the moon, but that's a small group."

Satisfied by my answer, we settled onto the blanket and chatted about the rest of Pride and Prejudice. Even though I hadn't finished, Amber had many thoughts and was eager to share them. I was more than happy to listen to her speak. The soft library light played across her features, high-lighting the curve of her cheek, the warmth in her eyes. The mating bond hummed between us, a constant reminder of what could be, and I itched to sink into it and bind her closer to me.

But I held myself in check. Amber had been hurt before. That much was clear. She needed time, and I would give her all the time in the world if it meant earning her trust. Though I feared I didn't have much time before nature demanded we solidify the bond.

"Xavier, tell me about yourself. Your family, your time here in Beastly Falls. Are you a gargoyle?"

Amber's question surprised me, broke the casual conversation we'd been enjoying up to this point. But I knew it had only been a matter of time before she asked for more about me. I hesitated before speaking, trying to find the words to share.

She laid a hand on my arm. "You don't have to share if you don't want to. I'm sorry if I pried."

I shook my head. "No, it's okay. Yes, I am the gargoyle on the library roof. My job, my purpose is to protect the library and the contents. Gargoyles are often tasked with a job, usually protection, which suits us well since we're strong and we have tough exteriors, able to handle challenges particularly well."

I flexed my arm and Amber touched me, feeling the rough skin that was harder than human skin when I was in my human form.

Amber ran her hands along my skin and squeezed my muscles. I braced myself for the hint of fear, but I saw none of that. "Your skin is rough, almost like stone. And it feels hard. But it's warmer than I expected."

I nodded. "I turn to stone during the day and, at night, I am more human-like, but my skin is still harder than yours, harder to damage. I also weigh more than you or another human of the same size, and can inflict more damage when I want to."

She continued to stroke me, her touch inflaming my senses. "You would be a formidable enemy. Do the library patrons require that much enforcement? Not returning books on time? Refusing to pay fines?"

Her comments were accompanied by a teasing grin and I knew she meant well, but it was a sore subject for me. "Most gargoyles protect towns or something more important, like Asa Graywing. My father was Beastly Falls protector before Asa."

"Why aren't you the Beastly Falls protector? Wouldn't you inherit the role from your father? Or does it not work like that?"

I shook my head. "My father abdicated his role before his death. He felt he could no longer serve in that role. I took on the role of library protector when the library benefactor, a minotaur named Jazan Gartus, asked me to do so. I have remained its guardian ever since."

"I think it's a worthy task. You have so many valuable books in the collection here. Someone might try to steal them," Amber said.

How could I explain the shame I felt? Gargoyles were strong protectors, meant for greater things, yet I could only protect a building since my father had failed to protect the ill-fated couple who caused the town's curse. His failure was mine, and my mother never let either of us forget it.

"What happened to your mother? Is she still alive?"

"She died ten years ago. My father shortly after her," I replied shortly, not knowing how to explain the relief I felt at their passing, even as it left me alone in the world.

Amber made a sound of sympathy. "I'm so sorry for your loss. Did you have any brothers or sisters?"

"No, I was an only hatchling. My mother's clan came from another town, and my father was clanless. They fell in love and moved here many years ago."

Had that been the root of my mother's discontent? Even as a child, I remember her being unhappy, never pleased with anything my father did. He had been a protector for the town, much like Asa Graywing was now. She resented how much time he spent guarding the town, but she never liked when he was home either. Then, when he failed to protect the star-crossed couple and the curse struck, she found herself trapped in Beastly Falls, trapped with a failure for a mate and a child of that bloodline, as she often reminded me.

How could I share that with Amber? How could I share I was the reason she was trapped here in Beastly Falls, even before the curse? If she hadn't had offspring, she could have left. But once I came along, she remained, only to become a victim of the curse.

"That's so romantic," Amber breathed.

Amber was a good female, kind and gentle. But she didn't understand. "It was not like one of your novels, Amber. They should have never mated or had a hatchling. My mother resented my father, resented me, and once the curse trapped her here, her anger and bitterness poisoned her and everyone around her until she finally died from it. Not every story has a happy ending. I know that, more than most."

I couldn't help but wonder if I was doomed to not have a happy ending too, or was I being teased with the possibility, with Amber right in front of me? Would she be taken from me, my happiness snatched away at the last moment?

She was quiet for a moment, her hand still on my arm, warm and soothing. "I understand why you avoid romance novels, Xavier. I think I would too, with a history like that. But I can't imagine your mother resenting you. And, if she did, she was wrong. You're a wonderful male, a good male. Shame on her for not seeing that."

Warmth spread through me at her words, and I cleared my throat through the burn of tears long unshed. I reached for the bottle of wine to top off our glasses. As I poured her a glass of wine, I allowed myself a moment of hope. Perhaps this evening, trapped together in the library, would be the beginning of something beautiful. Perhaps, just maybe, we could break not only my curse but hers as well, showing her that males can be trusted.

CHAPTER 8
AMBER

Xavier's history was so sad and I wanted to comfort him, only I didn't know how. Well, I did, but I wasn't sure I had the confidence to do so.

It had been a pleasant evening to that point. The initial panic that had consumed me when the doors locked had faded, replaced by a warmth that seemed to grow with each passing moment. Xavier's thoughtfulness in preparing this picnic, his patience, and the way he gave me space when I needed it went a long way to easing my fears.

When he shared information about his family, though, I felt his pain as a visceral reaction deep inside, almost as if I was experiencing it with him. My heart ached for the lonely boy rejected by his mother, watching his father fall into darkness as the curse took his town. No wonder I sensed sadness cloaking Xavier, despite him trying to be kind and protective.

I felt I owed him something in return, a sharing of information, and I wanted to. I wanted him to understand me and how I got here, even as I was embarrassed about how I had fallen into the situation with Kevin. But I wasn't ready yet. I was falling under his spell, feeling more for Xavier than anyone else I had ever met, and so quickly. It scared me, because every single time I fell for someone, they betrayed me. But I sensed I could trust Xavier.

"You scare me, Xavier." He started to pull away, but I grabbed his arm and held him in place. "Not in a bad way. Well, maybe it is. I'm not sure. You make me feel things that I swore I would never feel again. It's only been a couple of days and I already care for you, deeply. The last time I trusted my feelings, I got hurt. Badly."

Xavier cupped my cheek and stroked his thumb along my lower lip. "Amber, I'm not pushing for anything you're not ready for."

"You're too kind, Xavier. Almost too good to be true."

I sucked in a deep breath. I had to tell him about Kevin, about my reasons for being here. "I'm not sure how I got here. I've been on the run for a few months from my ex-boyfriend, Kevin. He started out so sweet. Sending me flowers, gifts, picking me up at work, taking me out to nice dinners. He seemed like a dream come true after so many loser boyfriends. He had a good job, a nice apartment, didn't play video games all the time, drinking beer and leaving clothes everywhere. He seemed like an adult."

Xavier grew still under my touch and I pulled my hand back, folding them in my lap in a rigid fist. "It started so slowly that I never saw it. I stopped seeing my friends, stopping going to happy hour at work. If there was a male clerk at a store, I would find another aisle or I would not make my purchases because he would accuse me of flirting with the clerk. At restaurants, I would pray we had a female server and if we had a male, I would ask Kevin to order for me and never look at the server. It never mattered. He always accused me of coming on to them."

A low rumble grew in Xavier's chest and, when I glanced over, he stopped. "Sorry. Please continue."

"The day he punched me in the stomach and backhanded me across the face, I left," I continued. "I didn't dare go home or to my friends. He'd isolated me by then and I didn't have any friends left I trusted. My family hated him and told me that I wasn't welcome if I was with him. Not to mention I was afraid of what he'd do to them. So I ran. But he followed. He always followed. I haven't felt safe since then, always moving, worried he'd hurt anyone I got close to. So, I just stopped making friends."

Silence reigned in the library for several minutes, then the glass in Xavier's hand shattered. I jumped and cried out. He quickly gathered up the shards of glass and cleaned the wine that had splattered everywhere, careful not to look at me.

I despaired the longer he avoided my gaze. Had I scared him away? I knew he could handle Kevin, but was I too messed up for him? Had I shared too much? I knew I should have kept my mouth shut. My situation was too fucked up for anyone to deal with.

Tears blinded my vision, and I began to clean up the food. Xavier's hand settled over mine. "Amber, stop. Please."

He tilted my chin to face him. "I'm sorry for not talking sooner. I was so angry, and I didn't want to scare you further. I didn't want you to think I was like that other male, that dishonorable male, but I scared you anyway. I'm sorry."

I blinked, clearing the tears from my vision. No one had ever apologized to me before. "You're sorry? You have nothing to be sorry for. I shouldn't have told you."

"No, you should have told me. If that male comes

61

anywhere near you, I will protect you. You're safe here. I promise. Whether by my hand or those here in Beastly Falls, he will never hurt you as long as you are here," he vowed.

"Maybe I'd better stay forever, then," I joked.

Xavier swallowed hard and avoided my gaze. "I hope you can, Amber."

I narrowed my gaze. His words seemed ominous, but I didn't understand. I had a job, a place to live. Why wouldn't I be able to stay? Though Anya had said my job was provisional for seven days. "What aren't you telling me, Xavier?"

He sighed and settled back on the blanket, staring up at the ceiling of the library that resembled the night sky. "You know about the curse, but you may not know everything. We have not found our fated mates because they're not here in town. Only recently have newcomers been allowed into town, allowed to find their mates."

I nodded, remembering something either he or Esme had told me. "I think you told me this before."

"But it's not that simple. They were trapped here for seven days until they accepted their mate, unable to leave until that time was done. If they do not accept their mate by the end of the time, they are expelled from Beastly Falls, unable to return."

My blood chilled. I might not be able to stay in Beastly Falls, even if I wanted, unless I accepted my mate? This had quickly become my sanctuary, the one place Kevin could not catch me. What would I do if I couldn't stay?

He settled his somber gaze on me. "Amber, you're my mate. You're the only one who can break my curse."

CHAPTER 9
XAVIER

I hadn't planned on telling Amber so bluntly that she was my mate. Had feared that it might scare her away, especially given her experiences with dishonorable males. The mate bond demanded that I make Amber mine, that I claim her and tie her to me so closely that she can never leave, thus breaking my curse. Yet, I could not lie to her, could not claim her with a lie between us. She needed to know the truth, needed to accept me and my curse, to make an informed choice. I would not take that decision from her, force her to live a life of exile in Beastly Falls, watch her wither and die like my mother had simply for having chosen the wrong male.

Amber pulled away from me, wrapping her arms around her bent knees and staring off into the stacks of books, but I sensed she wasn't seeing the books. I remained silent, letting her work through her feelings and thoughts at her own pace, yet a part of me wanted to demand that she speak with me, tell me what she was thinking.

After several long minutes, during which I despaired of

ever winning her, Amber turned to me. "How long have you known that I'm your mate?"

"I suspected when you first came to town, but I knew that first night when I met you."

"Is that why everyone kept coming in here, asking me out? They were hoping I was their mate, but they realized I was yours?"

"Yes. Everyone has been excited since there have been a few newcomers in recent weeks. It seems as if the curse is weakening," I admitted.

She fell silent and stared into the stacks again. I couldn't wait in this silence any longer. I had lived in a purgatory for many years waiting for my mate. Now she was sitting next to me and I had to know her thoughts.

"Amber, talk to me. Please," I steeled myself for her rejection, expected it really.

She faced me again. "I don't understand this curse. I don't even understand the whole fated mates thing, beyond what I've read in books. But I can't deny that I feel a connection with you. I'm just not sure I'm ready for that."

Disappointment stabbed me deep inside, but I expected it. No one had ever chosen me, not really. And Amber had only just come to town a couple of days ago. She barely knew me. She needed time to get to know me. Time we didn't have.

The lights dimmed in the library, and soft orchestral music played. Amber looked around. "Is someone in here with us?"

I laid a hand on her arm soothingly. "I would have heard if anyone had come in. I think the library did that."

"On its own? The library is a building, not a person," Amber protested.

"Is it?" I countered. "We may as well relax, since I don't think we're going anywhere soon."

I stood and held out a hand to her. "May I have this dance, milady?"

She blushed and took my hand, letting me help her to her feet. I pulled her close, and we moved into a slow dance, swaying gently to the beat of the music, letting the sound carry us away. Slowly, she relaxed in my arms, her muscles loosening, and she settled against me, her head on my shoulder. I held her close, my cheek against the softness of her hair, smelling the sweet fragrance of strawberries and vanilla and the scent of Amber. She was beautiful, curvy and luscious and all mine. She fit me perfectly, her curves against my hard angles, her head fitting just under my chin, her softness a contrast to my hardness. She was perfect, and I craved to pull her closer, claiming her as mine.

Yet I feared I would have to let her go. And I would, if she wanted it. I would never force Amber to stay if she didn't want to. She would have to make the choice willingly to stay, not because of guilt or threats.

Amber tilted her head, and I couldn't resist. I leaned down and brushed her lips with mine. Amber's lips were warm and soft against mine, the sensation sending a shiver down my spine. The connection between us was powerful, like two puzzle pieces finally clicking into place after waiting for so long.

I wrapped my arms wrapped around her, pulling her closer, my wings flaring to cocoon us in a shield of warmth and safety. She opened her mouth, her tongue darting out to tease mine, the taste of sweet wine combining with her own flavor exploding on my tongue. I groaned and crushed her closer, taking over the kiss in an instant.

As our kiss deepened, emotions flooded through me. My wings enveloped us, creating a sense of intimacy and protection that I had never experienced before. Her lips were insistent against mine, igniting a fire deep within me that I never knew existed. The taste of sweet wine lingered on my tongue, mixing with the heady sensation of desire that pulsed between us.

In that moment, hope flared again, and I believed that this bond of ours could have a chance of saving not only me but Amber, too. Her hands stroked over my body, the heat of her touch burning through my shirt, sending my heart racing. I desperately wanted to explore her soft skin, feel her tremble under me, but I held myself back, let her have this moment.

She paused, her hands hovering over my arms, and a low rumble escaped me, resonating through my body. Amber jerked back, her eyes wide.

"It's been so long since someone has touched me," I said roughly, gently taking her hand and bringing it back. "Please. Again."

I would have begged for her touch, fallen to my knees for another caress if she had stopped, but she didn't hesitate. She grew bolder with her explorations, her hands tracing the muscles on my chest and I longed to feel her soft skin over mine.

She reached up on tiptoes and brushed a lock of my dark hair from over my brow, then trailed her fingers over my face and down my neck until the place where my wings met my upper back. Her hands hesitated over the arch of one of my wings and she looked at me, hesitating.

"You can touch them, Amber. You can touch my anywhere." My voice was rough as if from disuse and her eyes flared with heat.

She settled her hand on a leathery wing and firm bone frame. I groaned as she stroked along the ridge, charting the upper edge of my wing, then down the side. As she brushed the surface, she asked. "How far can you fly?"

Visions of flying with Amber in my arms, kissing her, making love to her in the air made my cock painfully hard. "Pretty far, though I've never tested it since I can't leave the boundaries of Beastly Falls. I can take you flying some time, if you would like."

She sucked in a breath. "I'd like that."

I was dying for a taste of her, to bring her the same pleasure she was bringing me as she explored me, but this was for her, to gain her trust, to give her a chance to know me. But the night had to end. I sensed the sun on the rise and I would soon turn to stone. She needed time to think, time to decide her next steps. I would not force her into any decisions, not tonight, not any night. But we both needed space.

As if the library sensed the coming daylight, the music ended, and the lights brightened. Our time was drawing to a close. At least for this evening.

I cupped her cheek and stroked my thumb along her soft cheek one last time. "Our time tonight has ended. I hope you enjoyed your picnic."

A soft smile curved her lips. "I loved it, Xavier. Thank you so much."

She rose on her toes and brushed her lips with me, leaning in to deepen it, before pulling away with a regretful sigh. "I suppose we should clean this up before Anya or Evelyn see this."

"I'll take care of it. You check the desk and head for home. Good night, Amber."

She turned, giving me an impish smile. "Good night, Xavier. Thank you for the best date ever."

"No, Amber. Thank you for the best memory," I whispered after her departing figure. I would treasure this night, long after I turned to stone forever.

CHAPTER 10
AMBER

The next morning, I woke up around lunch time after a restless sleep, dreaming of Xavier's strong arms enfolding me, his firm body coming over me, his hard cock thrusting inside of me. I hadn't had a sex dream in years but this one was so realistic that I wondered if it had actually happened. Last night, I had been so close to asking him to take me to bed but then he ended our dance, the hints of pinks and oranges beginning to streak the morning sky. Fate cruelly ending our time together. But it was for the best. I needed some time to process everything that we discussed, especially the curse and the mating bond he'd shared with me.

Including the time limit, which terrified me. For the first time in months, I felt safe. Part of that was Beastly Falls itself. The town had a way of enfolding newcomers in and making you feel welcome. But the larger part was how Xavier made me feel. Safe, protected, loved. It was crazy that I had only known him for a few days. Could I really be considering staying?

My feelings for Xavier had come on so suddenly, so

69

intensely. The safety I felt with him, the attraction, was unlike anything I'd experienced before. But doubt nagged at me. My track record with men wasn't exactly stellar, and Xavier's protective gaze as I slept, uncomfortably echoed Kevin's obsessive behavior.

Esme had left me some sandwiches and a note the previous evening, reminding me that she had been out with her wolf pack, and apologizing for not being available for my after-shift meal. And this morning, she was also absent, probably recovering from her romp through the forest. I preferred to think of her as playing with her fellow wolves and not chasing down cute little bunnies or baby deer. I was fine with her not having a meal for me. I wanted to explore the town further.

So I headed down the walkway and onto Main Street, going straight for the Growling Bean and the best cup of coffee I'd had in weeks. Wyn Trafiel, a faun, for that's what he was as I now knew, was working the counter. He wore a white button-down shirt, an embroidered hunter green vest, and shorts over his goat legs, all giving him a slightly Germanic look. It was adorable, though not quite what I expected from the slightly hipster feel the cafe had.

He gave me a broad smile when I came in, his tufted ears twitching in his curly honey blond hair. "Welcome, Amber. What can I get you today?"

I scanned the handwritten menu in chalk on the blackboard on the wall. "Everything looks delicious. I'm famished. What can you recommend?"

He studied me for a long moment, his head cocked to the side, his eyes narrowed, and I swear he was actually reading me in some weird way. "A cup of our soup of the day with a grilled five-cheese sandwich on the side, and some extra bergamot Earl Grey tea with local honey. I think that would be perfect for you," he declared.

He was right. It sounded like the perfect lunch. "Excellent. I'll grab a seat by the window again?"

He nodded, and I headed for the window seat where I had first joined this odd little town and could people watch while I ate. Customers bustled about, all greeting me and wishing me a good day. No one was rude or unpleasant. Everyone seemed happy and friendly. I loved it.

Wyn brought my tea and food, and I settled in to eat. It was delicious. The soup was creamy and just a hint of tart tomato. The grilled cheese was crispy on the special bread and gooey with the cheeses all complemented each other. I devoured the meal ridiculously fast. Once I finished eating and was sipping my tea, a couple approached my table.

"Mind if we join you?" the woman asked, her smile warm. "I'm Jenny Cortado. I'm new to Beastly Falls, too."

I glanced up and saw a pleasant young woman with a friendly smile. Behind her was Rook Mullein, the vampire who was friends with Xavier. I smiled and gestured to the seat across from me.

"Of course. Rook, am I right?" Then I frowned. I thought vampires couldn't walk in sunlight. But that would be rude to ask, so I kept my mouth shut.

Jenny slid into the chair with a cup of coffee. She was clearly human, with a streak of grease on her shirt, which made me wonder what she did for work. Rook dragged over a chair from another table and sat on it.

He smiled, revealing two fangs. "It's nice to see you again, Amber. I'm glad you stayed in our fair town."

Jenny shot him a look. "She's the one you met at the library? Of course she was. Who else would be new to town?" Jenny rolled her eyes and faced me. "Rook told me he met you but didn't say too much, only that Xavier was interested in you. How do you like Beastly Falls? It's pretty cool, right?"

She was a force of nature, in all the right ways. Fun and easy to talk to. I liked her. "It's adorable. A bit quirky, but I like it."

Jenny laughed. "Quirky is putting it mildly. More like a major culture shock for those of us not from here. I mean, no cell phones? How does that work? Though I like not being constantly pinged for stuff. It's oddly relaxing."

"It's definitely different. I miss some of the newer books in the library and researching some topics on the computer. I haven't used a card catalog in years and their shelving system is not exactly the Dewey Decimal system."

Jenny grinned and leaned into Rook, clearly a woman in love. "But they make up for it in other ways. I'm opening a garage in town, restoring older cars, which works out since most of the cars here are older models. I'm on my lunch break, after working on a Toyota most of the morning. Need any work done on your car?"

"Mate, don't drum up business now," Rook chided gently.

"Oh, right. Sorry. Habit, you know? I always talk about cars. Like you probably talk about books, right?" Jenny shrugged.

There was something about their dropping by that pinged my radar. I couldn't shake the feeling that this impromptu meeting wasn't coincidental, especially since I had seen Rook a couple of times now since I came to town. But I'd play along.

"What are you reading?" I gave her a sly look and Rook laughed.

Jenny grimaced. "Walked into that one." She bit her lower lip, then continued, "So, you and Xavier."

I tensed, braced for an uncomfortable conversation. I wondered if they would warn me off or support us. Did they know we were mates? Of course, they had to know. Others in town knew it. Rook was his friend and would have to know.

"We've been spending some time together," I said cautiously.

Rook nodded soberly. "I've been friends with Xavier for many years. I assume you know about the town's curse and its effect on him."

"He mentioned the town curse and how he is stone during the day as a result until he meets his mate," I said, confused by the direction of the conversation. I wanted to ask if he was affected by it too, but wasn't sure how to broach the subject.

"Yes, he is fated to remain stone during the day until he meets his mate. Then, he could walk as a human all the time," he confirmed. "I too was cursed to be a nightwalker until I met Jenny. She is my true mate and broke my curse."

He looked at Jenny, his gaze filled with so much love that my heart clenched. I wanted that, had been looking for that forever. Instead, I found Kevin and my life turned into a nightmare. Yet, maybe I had a second chance.

I turned to Jenny, curious about her decision to remain in Beastly Falls. "Did you ever question staying with Rook?"

She laughed again, her hand on Rook's arm. "Of course. I had a job interview in New York and was headed there when my car broke down here, trapping me here for a few days. Despite falling for Rook, I didn't believe in love at first sight or fated mates or anything like that."

"But you stayed," I persisted.

She nodded. "I stayed. Rook is worth staying for. I love him. I couldn't imagine living my life without him. Besides, if I had left, he would have died."

The implication hung heavy in the air, and my blood chilled in my body. "What do you mean, died?"

"Once we find our fated mate," Rook said. "We must complete the bond, or the curse takes us. In my case, I could not feed from anyone but my mate. I would slowly starve to death without her."

I sat back, absorbing this new information. Xavier could die without me? Why didn't he tell me this when he told me about the curse?

"We suspect you might be Xavier's mate," Jenny said. "But he won't tell you because he's worried about forcing you into something you're not ready for."

I stared at Jenny and Rook. "He told me about the curse and the mate bond, but not this. Could Xavier die?"

They exchanged a look. "We don't know for sure. The curse affects everyone differently," Jenny said. "But there have only been a couple of mate bonds so far, when there have been none in over two decades. The town's curse might be weakening, possibly even breaking. If you and Xavier are truly mates, you could free him—and potentially help to free the whole town."

"But," Rook added firmly, "only if it's what you truly want. If you're not sure, if you don't feel the same, it would be kinder to leave now, before the bond has fully formed. That would let him be free to find someone else."

I stared into my tea, my reflection rippling in the rapidly cooling liquid. The intensity of my feelings for Xavier suddenly made sense, but was I ready for this kind of commitment? This kind of responsibility? We had not made love. Maybe we had not formed the bond yet, leaving both of us free to be separate and free. But he lied to me about the curse, about the impact on him. Why?

"Take your time," Jenny said softly. "But be gentle with Xavier. He's waited a long time for this possibility."

As they stood to leave, I found myself at a crossroads. Stay and potentially change not just my life, but an entire town's fate? Or run, as I had been doing for so long?

~

I wandered the town for the rest of the afternoon, enjoying the shops, visiting some of the residents, and thinking about when Jenny and Rook had shared with me. I only had a few days left to decide what I wanted to do. Was I ready to commit to Xavier for life, or did I walk away and give up this chance forever?

One thing I knew for certain. Xavier, while protective and caring, was not overbearing and controlling like Kevin. Nor was he immature and useless. He respected me, considered me and my feelings. And I was beginning to care for him very much. A girl could do worse. I should know. I had done worse. Much worse.

But that wasn't a reason to stay with someone forever, nor was it a reason to sleep with someone. Xavier was incredibly sexy. A strong male, with a protective streak that turned me on like nothing I ever expected. He had muscles for days, but never used his power to intimidate or get his way. His kindness and thoughtfulness drew me in like nothing I had ever experienced.

But more than that, every time I was near him, I could feel my body responding. My pulse pounded in my throat. My stomach fluttered like a kaleidoscope of butterflies. And my whole body went molten at the thought of being in his arms again. All I wanted was his touch, his kiss, his body over mine. The dream I had last night, or this morning really, only made me want him more.

I had a few days to spend with him before I had to decide about the mating, and I wasn't going to waste it. Tonight, I wanted to spend it with Xavier, satisfying my curiosity about how we could be together. Anya had given me the evening off, saying we all had two nights in a seven-day period off. I thought it was awfully quick to have a night off, but I wasn't complaining. Not when I had a mission.

I was going to seduce Xavier Chauvre.

CHAPTER II
XAVIER

T stretched gently, the stone slow to leave my body as the sun set in the distance. My body was stiff and sore after all the hours spent in a crouch on the roof, but I was eager to find Amber, make sure she was okay. I hadn't sensed any danger from her all day, but her side of the bond was unsettled, almost sad, and I wondered why. I needed to know if she had changed her mind about me.

Finally, my body was loose enough for me to move and I stretched my wings to their full length, ready to fly to the ground, when I sensed someone behind me. I turned to see Amber sitting in the chair that Rook had brought up when he waited for me to return to human form. She was wrapped in a soft, gray, fuzzy blanket and sipping a cup of hot chocolate. She stared off into the sunset, not aware that I was watching her.

Her cheeks were reddened from the cool dusk air and the breeze that blew harder on top of the library. Her red, wavy hair was tousled by that same wind, giving her a just woke up look. I couldn't wait to see her look like that after a night in my bed, if I was lucky enough to have her in my bed.

"Amber?"

She turned a startled look at me, then a brilliant smile. "I hope you don't mind me waiting for you. I'm off tonight and thought I would return the favor with dinner. Unless you'd prefer breakfast."

She bit her lower lip in a sudden attack of nerves. Gratitude and hope filled me, a tingling through my chest and my whole body. She thought of me and considered my needs. A true mate.

I strode over to her and knelt in front of her, taking her icy hands in mine. "It's perfect. Let's eat in my quarters where it's warmer."

She gave me a startled look. "You have quarters here?"

I chuckled and got to my feet, tugging her up. "I do, in the library's basement. Come, let me show you."

I led her through the secret back corridors of the Beastly Falls library, down to the basement level where I kept my quarters, a hidden chamber known only to me and a few friends. I didn't need any interruptions for this private moment, even if the library appeared to be on our side. I couldn't trust someone would shatter our bubble. In my space, I could keep us safe, protect us, and seal our bond.

Pushing open the heavy oak door, we stepped into a room bathed in a soft, ethereal light that danced off the stone walls lined with ancient tomes. The air was thick with the scent of old parchment and magic, wrapping around us like a comforting embrace.

Amber's eyes widened in wonder as she took in the sight before her. "What is this place?" she asked, her voice hushed in reverence.

"This is where I come to be human," I replied, my tone

tinged with vulnerability. "Where I shed my stone skin and embrace my true form. This is my home."

She whirled around, taking in the space. "I love it! It's beautiful!"

I laid out the dinner she'd brought, and we ate a delicious dinner from the Spicy Demon, a blend of eastern ethnic foods run by a local demon. He was originally from the Far East and brought his love of cooking and the food to Beastly Falls. I loved the restaurant and Rook and I often went there once a week or so. It pleased me that Amber appeared to enjoy the same foods, especially judging by the sounds she made when she ate her dinner.

When we were done, Amber settled back in her chair, avoiding the elephant in the room, namely my king-sized bed, appropriately sized to accommodate my wings. I rarely slept in it now that I was stone all day on the roof, but I came here to be alone and to think. The bed was comfortable for when I wanted to rest.

"I've been thinking about what we talked about last night. The mating. Our bond. The curse."

I held my breath, worried that I was about to lose her, to hear the words I dreaded. I braced myself. "Yes, Amber?"

"I'm ready. I want to be yours."

"**M**ake me yours," she whispered, taking my hand and leading me to the king-sized bed in the center of the room.

I trailed after her, my heart racing with a mix of lust and anticipation. I felt nervous, vulnerable, and exposed. But with Amber, it felt natural, like revealing the deepest parts of myself to someone who truly understood.

As we stood by the bed, she turned to face me, her eyes searching for any hint of hesitation. Finding none, she slowly undid the buttons of my shirt, her fingers working quickly and expertly to reveal the skin beneath the human clothes that had shifted with me from stone to human.

I couldn't tear my gaze away from her, watching as her hands moved with such tenderness and reverence over my chest, tracing every muscle and curve that had been concealed for so long. When she finally pushed the fabric off my shoulders and let it fall to the floor, I shivered at the sudden rush of cool air, replaced by the heat of her touch.

Electricity coursed through my veins as Amber's lips left a trail of hot kisses along my chest, igniting a fire within me. Her eyes glinted with desire and I pulled her close, our bodies fitting together as if we were made for each other. Each touch set my body ablaze, instinct taking over as we explored each other with wild abandon.

I grabbed her hands as they drifted lower to my jeans. "Stop, or this will be over before we've even started."

She laughed, but the sound faded at the intensity in my gaze. I tilted her chin up and claimed her lips in a deeply possessive kiss, letting my inner beast rise to the surface. The male inside claiming his mate. Instead of being put off or backing away, she arched into me, her lips opening under my kiss, her tongue tangling with mine. No hesitation whatsoever.

Amber humbled me with her trust, her passion, her openness to taking chances with her heart. I wanted to be worthy of her, to make this night even more special than I already had, to show her what she meant to me. And hopefully, she would accept the mate bond and end my curse.

I cupped the back of her head and angled her to deepen the kiss, my fingers tangling in her silky auburn hair, holding her in place while I took control of the moment. Our tongues mated, stoking the heat of our desire, her taste both sweet and uniquely Amber. My blood burned hot, racing in my veins, pushing me to claim her.

I trailed kisses along her jawline, then down her neck. She let her head fall back, moaning as I sucked along her pounding pulse point, licking the salty skin.

I growled as her shirt got in my way, and her hands came up to the collar. "Don't damage my clothes. I don't have many clean ones right now."

"I'll buy you new ones," I growled.

She stepped back and quickly stripped out of her clothes, her shirt going one way and her tailored black pants the other way. My mouth went dry as she stood before me, clad only in a simple white lace bra and panty set that somehow seemed sexy for all its simplicity. I drank in the sight of her, her beauty, the freckles that dotted her creamy skin like stars in the night sky, her full breasts, her gently rounded hips. I didn't know where to begin my exploration. The gods willing, I had years to learn everything about her.

She planted her hands on her hips and arched an eyebrow at me. "Excuse me. I'm feeling a little lonely here." I smiled and took a step forward, intended to show her how I felt, but she held up a hand. "Hang on, buddy. You're a little overdressed. Strip and do it slowly."

She perched on the edge of the bed, almost primly, like the librarian that she was, triggering a new fetish that I hadn't realized I had.

My shirt was already off so I kicked off my boots and stepped out of my jeans, putting them on top of the chair on the side. I slowly pivoted to see Amber's eyes wide, her mouth slightly opened. She was staring at my cock with a mix of trepidation and excitement.

She swallowed hard and reached for me, her hands barely circling my girth. She stroked my length, exploring me with tentative touches, then more confident strokes.

She looked up at me, her hazel eyes darkening to a green. She licked her lips and reached for me, pulling me down. "Love me. Make me forget everything."

CHAPTER 12
AMBER

I have to admit, when Xavier first got undressed, which had to be the most unsexy striptease I had ever seen, I almost swallowed my tongue. Kevin, nor any of my previous boyfriends, had ever been well-endowed by any stretch of anyone's imagination, though they thought they were the cocks of the walk. They could barely handle themselves, much less get a girl off. And forget about directions. Even with directions, GPS, a map and a tutor, he couldn't find my clit, a g-spot or anything else to bring me to the promised land. And he sure as hell never knew the difference between me faking it or the real thing, not that I ever experienced the real thing with him unless it was by accident, though fantasies about Thor or Iron Man, and a judicious use of some toys or my fingers.

Xavier was definitely bigger than I expected, and one question was answered when I explored him. He was not rough stone as the rest of them, but more like smooth marble. He was hard, but smooth, and definitely larger than I expected. But, based on how considerate he'd been about my feeling so far, I suspected he knew how to use it to bring a girl some serious joy. And I was eager to get this show on the road.

Xavier followed me onto the bed, and he took over. He took my wrists in one hand and pinned them over my head. "No touching."

He took my lips in another deep kiss, but didn't linger there for long. He nibbled down my throat again, reigniting the heat that burned inside of me, flaring to life again. I arched into his kiss, silently begging for him to move lower, to stop teasing me, and he accommodated me. He traced his dark tongue along the lace of my bra, teasing the edges, dipping between the mounds and up the other side. Finally, he sucked a tip into his mouth through the lace, and I moaned loudly. The sensation of his hot breath on my sensitive skin combined with the friction of the lace was too much.

I shifted beneath him, trying to get closer, but he held me steady. "No," he growled, and it sent a shiver down my spine. "I'm in charge here."

His fingers deftly undid the clasp at the back, and I gasped as he dragged it away from my body. He caught his breath as he looked down at my bared chest, and desire blazed in his eyes. He released my hands, and I buried them in his hair, tugging him close.

"You are so beautiful," he murmured, and then he leaned down again, taking one nipple into his mouth.

The feeling of his teeth gently scraping against my skin while his tongue danced around my sensitive peak sent waves of pleasure coursing through me. I arched up into him again, pleading for him to continue. He complied gladly, switching to my other breast and showering it with the same intensity. I gripped the sheets beneath me, my fingers digging in as the sensations built up inside me.

As he continued his exploration, my heart pounded, and my emotions were a whirlwind of desire and uncertainty. My thoughts kept going back to the question of what this meant for us – for our future together. But for now, all that mattered was the heat of his body pressing against mine, the gentle sound of his breathing, and the feel of his skin against mine.

Xavier's hands moved lower, tracing a path over my belly, down to my hips, and then continuing even lower. He spread my legs open further, exposing me to him completely. I felt him position himself at my entrance, his cock feeling impossibly large.

"Are you ready?" he asked in a gruff voice, his eyes locked onto mine as he readied himself.

I nodded, unable to speak past the lump in my throat. "Yes," I whispered.

He smiled, a hint of relief mixed with desire in his eyes. "I've got you," he said, his voice deep and smooth as he slowly pushed inside me.

He went slowly, gently, letting me adjust to his size. He was easily the largest male I had been with and, as I stretched to accommodate him, I worried it wouldn't fit. He paused, his eyes fixed on me, then his hand worked its way between us to rub against my clit, the sensation sending shockwaves through me. I gasped and tightened against him; the climax ripping through me unexpectedly.

When I came down from the sharp orgasm, Xavier was waiting patiently, watching me with a smirk on his face. He tenderly brushed the hair from my face and kissed me. "Ready?"

I couldn't imagine it getting any better, but I nodded. He advanced further, helped by my recent orgasm. The sensation was overwhelming, both pleasurable and a bit painful at first, but he moved slowly, giving me time to adjust. As he moved deeper inside me, I relaxed around him, our bodies melding together, the heat of our passion igniting something within me that I had never felt before. Finally, he was fully seated, and he pulled out, the friction making my eyes roll back in my head. He repeated the motion, and I moaned as he hit spots that I had only read about.

"Harder," I moaned, unable to resist the urge to pull him closer. He obliged, thrusting into me with renewed vigor. Each movement brought with it a wave of pleasure that washed over me, leaving me breathless and eager for more. His eyes never left mine, as if he wanted to make sure I was still with him, still enjoying this intimate moment we shared. And I was. With every thrust, every touch, every kiss, I felt myself sinking deeper into him, into this world of pure bliss that I never wanted to leave.

The rhythm of our lovemaking quickened, the sounds of our passion filling the room.

"You're amazing," he murmured again, his voice rough with emotion. "I've waited so long for this. So long for you, my mate."

I gripped him tighter, feeling the muscles in his body tensing as he pushed deeper within me. His hands held me steady, his touch both gentle and possessive. The sensation was overwhelming—a mix of pleasure and fulfillment that I had never experienced before. I felt a surge of warmth in my core, building up into a climax that threatened to consume me entirely. I knew it was close, just on the horizon, and I whimpered softly as it grew closer.

"That's it," Xavier whispered in my ear, his voice full of passion and desire. "Let go. Let me take care of you."

My eyes remained locked with his as the world around

me faded away, leaving just us in this moment of pure ecstasy. Xavier's movements grew more frantic, each thrust pushing me closer and closer to the edge.

And then it happened. A wave of pure bliss washed over me, consuming me entirely as I cried out his name in pleasure. Xavier groaned in response, his body shuddering against mine as he found his release within me. His murmured words of love and devotion filled the air, wrapping around us like a cocoon of emotion.

As we came down from our peaks, I wrapped my arms around him tightly, treasuring the feel of his skin against mine. Our hearts beat in unison, pulsing with the same rhythm of passion and love that now connected us forevermore.

Xavier traced gentle kisses along my jawline and down to my neck, as he slowly pulled away from me. I shivered at his touch, feeling completely drained and yet rejuvenated all at once. This was something new for me, something I had never experienced before.

He tucked me against his body, gently stroking my skin, the roughness of his fingers making me shiver. "Are you all right?" he asked softly, his voice full of concern. "You're quiet."

"I'm just trying to process everything. It was amazing."

He nodded. "I know it's a lot to take in," he said gently. "The mate bond makes everything more powerful, stronger. But I want you to know that I am here for you, no matter what you decide."

The mate bond. Damn it. I had forgotten about that. Did having sex now meant we were bonded together? That we could never be apart? I didn't know how I felt about that. I hadn't really thought that far ahead and wasn't sure

I was ready for a lifetime commitment, not when my life was such a chaotic mess so far.

As if interpreting my panic, Xavier pulled me closer and leaned down to press a soft kiss against my forehead. "The bond is not final. You still have a choice before you."

"So we didn't finalize anything?" I found that hard to believe. I never had an experience like I had with Xavier before. Sex had always been good, but not great. Not almost transformative, as this felt. It had to mean something.

He gave me a sad smile. "Accepting the mate bond involves more than having sex. There has to be a conscious choice, a decision on your part to accept the bond."

A wave of relief swept over me. I wasn't ready to accept the bond, not without understanding what it meant. And I still couldn't believe that I got swept away by my emotions so quickly, jumping into bed with Xavier so quickly. That was so not like me. Something magical was afoot.

"I'm glad to hear that. Not that I am rejecting you. I just need more time. We have seven days, right?" I asked, figuring now was as good a time as any to confirm the details of the curse.

He glanced away. "Yes, you have a week. At the end of that time, if the bond is not complete, you will be banished."

His tone was flat, not the soft, romantic one that I had become accustomed to for this evening. And it bothered me. "You haven't told me how it will affect you if we don't complete the bond."

He smiled at me then, a sad look that somehow also seemed brave. "The sun is rising. I need to return to the roof. We should clean up before the morning shift arrives."

And as the first light of dawn filtered through the small window, casting its golden hue over us, I felt like Xavier had ducked my question. Rook and Jenny told me what Xavier gained through the mating and what the curse would cost Rook if it failed. Could Xavier die? Why wouldn't he tell me?

"I know the curse can cause death. Rook told me that. Can it do that to you?" I insisted.

Xavier paused without looking at me. "Rook shouldn't have interfered. It doesn't cause death. It only magnifies our natures. In Rook's case, he would only be able to drink Jenny's blood. With her gone, he would starve."

I stepped in front of Xavier, forcing him to look at me. "And in your case?"

"I turn to stone."

CHAPTER 13
XAVIER

In the aftermath of our lovemaking, the mate bond throbbed inside of me, demanding that I seal the claim. But hearing Amber's reservations and fears about solidifying the claim made my blood run cold. It was as I feared. She regretted our bonding, was hesitating to complete our connection. I only had seven days to convince her to be my mate, and we had already wasted three of them. Even with the library's help, I could not persuade her to see me as a potential mate. What more could I do?

I felt the mate bond thrumming through my veins, urging me to complete it, to seal my connection with Amber and finally break free from this centuries-old curse. Doubt gnawed at me. How could I burden her with this? Trap her in Beastly Falls, bind her to me out of obligation rather than love?

Amber dressed quietly, her brow furrowing as she studied my face. "What are you thinking about?" she asked softly. "Do you regret what we did?"

I pulled her close, my heart aching at the vulnerability

in her voice. "Of course not," I assured her, even as I despaired. "I just want to be sure you're okay."

She was quiet for a moment, then nodded. "Yes, I am."

I remembered her past, her story of her ex-boyfriend and how few friends she had. She knew no one in Beastly Falls and had no support. She was more like my mother in that she would leave everyone behind if she stayed, be isolated. I couldn't do that to her. I couldn't be like that dishonorable male in her life. In that moment, I knew I couldn't complete the bond. Not yet. Amber needed to heal, to find her strength again, to build friendships and a support system. I couldn't be her entire world; that wouldn't be fair to either of us. Even if it meant we never completed the bond, that she would never be ready. She needed to be safe. She was the most important person, not me.

As if she read my mind, Amber asked, "I still feel you're not telling me everything. I'm sorry that I can't bond with you yet. Do you understand why?"

I cupped her cheek, feeling the soft skin under my palm. "Of course. I would never ask you to do anything that isn't right for you. I would never rush you."

"But the deadline..." she said.

"Don't worry about me. I'll be fine."

I would be fine. I would stay the silent sentry overlooking the library of Beastly Falls. I would never see Amber again, since she would be banished from the town, but I would fade from consciousness and not remember her. The pain would ease in time. I would survive. Eventually. Turning to stone, not just my exterior but every part of me, including my heart.

"What aren't you telling me?"

She persisted in her questions, but I refused to tell her

the entire truth. That I would be stone forever. I wouldn't lay that guilt on her. It wasn't her burden to bear.

"It's nothing. I just want to get back to my post before I turn to stone. It really sucks to be stone here in my quarters," I joked, but it fell flat when she eyed me suspiciously.

She sighed and helped me clean up. As we finished dressing, I felt her eyes on me, filled with questions I wasn't ready to answer. How could I explain the full extent of my curse, the loneliness of years spent as stone, when she was still processing the reality of our supernatural world?

For now, I would give her time. Time to adjust to the truth about me and about Beastly Falls. And maybe, in time, I would find the courage to tell her everything—about the mate bond, about my hopes for us, about the possibility of breaking the curse together.

But not yet. Not when everything was still so new and fragile between us.

CHAPTER 14
XAVIER

As the last rays of sunlight faded, I felt the familiar shift from stone to flesh. But something was off. An unsettling feeling churned in my gut, one I couldn't quite place.

"About time you woke up," a dry voice said from behind me.

I turned to see Rook stretched out in a chair that he kept here for those times when he visited me near the edge of the roof. His presence at this hour was unusual, and I sensed immediately that something was wrong.

"What is it?" I asked, stretching out my stiff limbs.

He fixed me with a serious stare. "Why didn't you tell me that you and Amber already slept together?"

I paused for a moment, then continued my gentle exercise to regain my motion, but it seemed harder tonight, the stone not leaving my muscles willingly. "I wasn't aware that you were keeping track of my sex life. I don't ask you about yours."

He pushed up from the chair and came to stand by the edge of the roof, peering down at the street below. "That's not the point and you know it. Amber might be your mate. The risks are too high for you to be moving this fast."

I slowly straightened, feeling my body resisting the movement, as if it wanted to remain a statue longer. "Weren't you the one who encouraged me to pursue her, to form a bond with her? Why the sudden change of heart?"

He faced me, his expression troubled. "I'm worried you're moving too fast. She might not be ready for this, Xavier."

I sighed, running a hand through my hair, shaking loose some stray gray bits of stone and ignoring the sense of unease that was growing. "It's too late for that."

His gaze sharpened on the dust that scattered from my hands. "Are you positive? Has the bond formed?"

"We've made love," I admitted. "The bond has formed, even if it's not complete. My fate is in her hands now."

Rook cursed under his breath. "You have to tell her the truth. About what it means for you if she rejects the bond. She asked us about it, but we avoided it."

I shook my head vehemently. "No. I won't trap her here, condemn her to a life of misery unless she chooses it willingly. I refuse to watch another woman waste away and become bitter, like my mother did after the curse locked us away."

"You're making a mistake," Rook argued. "Maybe she'll surprise you. Amber's stronger than you give her credit for."

"I'm not taking her choice away from her. And I forbid you or Jenny from getting involved," I said firmly. "End of discussion."

Rook opened his mouth to argue further, but something caught his eye. I followed his gaze to the town's entrance, where a car I didn't recognize was slowly rolling in. Another new presence in Beastly Falls? Unlike the others, this didn't feel like a positive addition to the town, but something, or someone, more ominous.

My mouth went dry and my heart pounded in my throat. Something about that car, about its presence here, felt wrong. Very wrong.

"You don't think...," Rook said slowly.

I didn't let him finish the thought. My mind was already racing, filled with possibilities, none of them good.

"We need to find Amber," I said, my voice tight with urgency. "Now."

As we made our way down from the roof, that feeling of disquiet grew stronger. Whatever was coming, I had a sinking feeling it was about to change everything. And not for the better.

I rushed to the library, Rook's words echoing in my mind. He was right; I needed to tell Amber the truth. But first, I needed to make sure she was safe. As I pushed open the heavy doors, the sight before me made my heart sink.

Amber sat at the circulation desk. One of the local werewolves, Nigel Rovell, leaning on the desk, flirting outrageously. He had been looking for his mate as long as the rest of us, but he had always respected the bonds that formed, not bothering Jenny or any of the other newcomers to town once a bond had begun. With the werewolf's sense of smell, he had to know Amber was mine. Yet, here he was, clearly making a move on my mate, in my territory, his hand touching hers.

And Amber was laughing at something he said.

Rage clouded my brain, and a red haze filled my vision.

"Xavier, I think you should back off. Right now."

Rook's worried voice came as if from a great distance, but I ignored him. This male dared to move in on my mate, dared to touch her in front of me. He had to die. Slowly, painfully. And I had to claim Amber. Immediately.

I heard a rumble and realized it came from my chest. Rook muttered something that sounded like, "Oh shit."

I stalked to the desk, and Amber looked up, a bright smile that faded to alarm. Nigel straightened and froze, as if scenting a higher predator advancing on him.

"Whoa, Xavier. I was only talking to her. She was recommending a book for me to read."

"In all my years of guarding the library, you have never once come in here. Why now? You dare steal my mate? In front of me?" I turned to Amber. "You prefer him over me?"

Amber's eyes were wide, her face pale. "I was showing him books on how to repel garden gnomes. They're stealing his vegetables."

I scoffed. "He's a werewolf. He only eats meat."

Nigel frowned. "That's not true. We eat all kinds of food, just like you."

I whirled on him and he took a couple of steps backwards, his hands up in surrender. "Sorry, Xavier. I'll come back and talk with Anya or Evelyn. Sorry!"

He scurried out of the library, never turning his back on me. When the door slammed shut behind him, I turned back to Amber. She no longer looked terrified. Now she looked pissed. The rest of the patrons were staring at us.

Rook stepped up and took my arm. "I think you should step away, give yourselves some time and space."

"What the hell was that about, Xavier?"

As soon as Amber spoke, I knew I had screwed up. The fog of anger had lifted and, when I looked at Amber, I realized she was furious with me. Her face was pale, with two red spots on her cheeks. Tears filled her eyes and her lower lips quivered.

"I'm sorry, Amber. I don't know what came over me." I took a tentative step forward, but she held up a hand and stepped back.

"It was the mate bond. It makes you a little crazy," Rook offered helpfully.

I shot him a look. "Thanks, but I have this."

Amber folded her arms in front of her. "Do you? Because what I saw was a crazy possessive asshole trying to control my life. Do you really trust me so little? I just got away from someone like that. I told you I didn't want someone else like that. I thought you were different, Xavier."

I dropped my hands, and my shoulders slumped. I was losing her. I had fucked up and drove her away. "I don't know what happened. I thought he was harassing you."

She shook her head. "No, you thought we were flirting. You never even asked me what was going on. And when I explained, you ignored me. Do you know how that made me feel?"

When her gaze met mine, the anguish and betrayal in her eyes confirmed my fears. I had lost her and my chance for a mate.

"Amber," I began, my voice barely above a whisper.

The fury that flashed across her face was like a physical blow. "I told you that I had just gotten out of a terrible relationship," she said, her voice rising. "I should have known better. This isn't going to work, Xavier. I have to go."

Her words cut deep, but I couldn't bring myself to fight. She was right. I was no better than that dishonorable male from her past. She was better off without me. I felt myself shutting down, retreating behind walls built over centuries of loneliness. I couldn't even tell her the life, or non-life, she was condemning me to. I loved her too much to trap her here.

"I understand," I said, my voice hollow. "Go. Be free, with my blessing."

Without waiting for her response, I turned and left the library. Each step away from her felt like agony, but I forced myself to keep moving. I had promised myself I wouldn't trap her, wouldn't force her into a life she didn't choose.

Even if it meant condemning myself to an eternity of stone.

As the library doors closed behind me, I wondered if I had just made the biggest mistake of my very long life.

CHAPTER 15
AMBER

As the library door closed behind Xavier, my chaotic maelstrom of emotions threatened to overwhelm me. Betrayal, anger, and fear warred within me. How could he have kept something so monumental from me? I literally held his life in my hands, and he hadn't thought to mention it? Yet, even when pushed to the wall, he refused to state it outright, refused to push me into accepting the bond, even out of guilt. Even as a small part of me wanted to give me credit for that, the rest of me held firm. He lied, manipulated me, and I had been there, done that, had plenty of scars from the experience. Never again.

Fuming, I began shoving books back onto shelves with more force than necessary. My mind raced, already planning to leave Beastly Falls. I hated the idea of running again, but I'd already stayed too long. This place, these people - they were becoming too important to me. And that was dangerous.

Evelyn was still in the library, working on some special project. I couldn't bring myself to face her, to explain why I was leaving. Instead, I scribbled a hasty resignation note for Anya and left it on her desk.

Taking a deep breath to steady myself, I approached Evelyn. "Hey, I'm not feeling well," I lied, hating how easily the words came. I told myself it wasn't a lie, not really. "I think I need to head home."

Evelyn looked up, concern etched on her face. She didn't seem entirely convinced, but nodded. "Of course, Amber. Take care of yourself, okay?"

I nodded, not trusting myself to speak further. Grabbing my bag, I headed for the side door, eager to escape into the night and figure out my next move.

As I pushed the door open, the cool night air hit my face. For a brief moment, I felt a pang of regret. Despite everything, a part of me didn't want to leave.

But before I could dwell on that thought, a hand clamped over my mouth. Strong arms grabbed me from behind. I tried to scream, to fight, but it was useless.

The last thing I saw was the library door swinging shut behind me as everything faded to black.

I woke with a pounding headache, disoriented and groggy. As my vision cleared, I realized I was in the back seat of a stopped car, filled with trash and detritus of a life on the run. Food wrappers, empty coffee cups, and bags discarded in the back seat as if it were the garbage heap. I knew this car. I always hated how messy it was. Since I had gone on the run, Kevin had basically lived out of his car, adding more trash to the backseat. And now he added me. Was he going to discard my body like so much trash when he was done?

I moved my head minutely, enough to see the stopped vehicle was surrounded by dense woods, dark and heavy. Yet, through the cracked windshield, I could see the welcome sign for Beastly Falls. Sunlight shone on the sign, so it must be morning. How long had I been unconscious?

When I realized I was alone in the car, I cautiously sat up, trying to get my bearings, searching for a way to escape. My hands and feet weren't bound. I had just been tossed in the backseat and covered with trash as camouflage. My mouth was dry and my head pounded. I prayed for it to clear because I knew I had to be ready to run, despite the dizziness and fatigue that plagued my muscles.

Someone kicked the tires and began yelling at the front of the vehicle. I looked between the front seats to see that the front of the car was crumpled, as if it had hit an invisible wall. And there, pacing wildly by the hood, was Kevin. Blood trickled from a cut on his forehead, his face contorted with rage as he kicked the tires and gestured frantically.

"Damn it!" he shouted. "Why can't we leave this freakish town?"

He then turned and seemed to pound on an invisible wall. Was he high? Doing some weird new drug that was giving him hallucinations? I couldn't see anything, but clearly something was preventing Kevin from moving forward. Oh my God, was he someone's fated mate? I couldn't imagine it. Everyone in town was so nice. Who could be tied to Kevin forever? However, maybe he was drawn here because of me and he wasn't someone's fated mate. Maybe I brought Kevin to Beastly Falls and was the reason he could slip through the barrier.

My heart raced as I assessed the situation. Kevin hadn't noticed I was awake yet. Slowly, carefully, I eased the door open and slipped out.

The moment my feet touched the ground, Kevin whirled around, his eyes wild and angry. Our eyes met, the car sitting between us like a flimsy barrier. Oh, the hell with this. I was just done with being afraid, being chased by this man-child who couldn't get over me and our relationship.

"Why?" I demanded, my voice shaking. "Why can't you just let me go?"

His face twisted with rage, turning what I once thought was a handsome man to an ugly monster, which was an insult to the creatures inhabiting Beastly Falls. "You took everything from me! I just wanted to love you. Why couldn't you just love me back?" He ran a hand through his hair, leaving streaks of blood. "You reported me for stalking. I lost my job because of you! After everything I gave you!"

"You beat me!" I shouted back, anger overriding my fear. "You terrified me, isolated me from everyone I cared about. You threatened my family and friends. That's not love, Kevin."

"I did it to protect you!" he insisted.

Suddenly, a realization hit me like a bolt of lightning. "If you truly loved me, you would have set me free."

In that moment, Xavier's face flashed in my mind. Xavier, who had let me go, knowing it could kill him. That was true love.

Without hesitation, I turned and sprinted into the woods, back towards Beastly Falls, towards Xavier and the love that waited for me. I heard Kevin's enraged shout behind me, followed by the sound of him crashing through the underbrush in pursuit.

My heart pounded as I ran, branches whipping at my face. I had to make it back to town. Back to Xavier. I just hoped I wasn't too late.

CHAPTER 16
XAVIER

I stood atop the library, a stone sentinel once more. But this time, the familiar weight of my granite form felt like a prison. Despair filled every crevice of my being, as unyielding as the stone that encased me.

The previous night had been a blur of frantic searching. Amber was gone, vanished without a trace. I couldn't sense her through our nascent mating bond. The truth was undeniable - she had rejected me and left Beastly Falls. With her departure, my fate was sealed.

As the sun climbed higher in the sky, I wondered if this would be my last day of awareness. Would I ever wake again, or would I remain a lifeless statue for eternity? The thought should have terrified me, but I felt only a dull ache of acceptance.

Suddenly, a jolt of panic and fear surged through me. But these emotions weren't mine. They were Amber's. She was in trouble, desperate for help. The realization hit me like a physical blow. She needed me, and I was trapped in this cursed form, unable to move, to speak, to even cry out.

I strained against my stone prison with every ounce of

will I possessed. If I could just move a finger, blink an eye, anything to signal for help. But it was useless. I remained frozen, a silent witness to Amber's distress.

The bond between us pulsed with her fear, growing stronger with each passing moment. She was getting closer to town, I realized. Running towards Beastly Falls, towards me.

But I was powerless to help her. As her terror mounted, so did my frustration and despair. For the first time in centuries, I truly felt the weight of my curse. To be so close, yet so hopelessly far from the one I loved in her moment of need. It was a special kind of torment.

All I could do was wait, a stone gargoyle with an all-too-human heart, silently praying for Amber's safety and for the sun to set so I could finally come to her aid.

As I struggled against my stone prison, a shimmering figure materialized before me. Ethereal and barely visible in the daylight, it regarded me with ancient, knowing eyes.

"What would you give up for Amber?" the spectral being asked, its voice echoing in my mind rather than in the air.

Without hesitation, I answered, "I would give up anything to save her."

The figure cocked its head, as if I was a puzzle it could not understand. "Would you give up your life?"

Again, there was no delay in my answer. "Gladly. If it meant keeping her safe."

The figure nodded slowly, a hint of sadness in its other-worldly features. "I will grant your wish," it intoned. "You can be human and save her, but know this: she has until nightfall to accept the bond, or you will remain a statue forever."

The weight of this ultimatum settled heavily upon me.

It was a steep price, with no guarantee of success. But Amber's fear still pulsed through our bond, spurring me to action.

"I accept," I said, my determination unwavering.

Suddenly, I felt a crack. Then another. The stone encasing me began to splinter and crumble. With a surge of strength I didn't know I possessed, I pushed against my granite prison. Chunks of rock fell away, clattering on the library roof.

In a final, dramatic burst, I broke free. Human flesh replaced stone, and I stumbled forward, gasping in the sunlight I hadn't felt on my skin in centuries.

There was no time to marvel at this miracle. Amber needed me. With renewed purpose, I flew off the roof, skimming the ground before I caught a draft.

As I flew towards the forest where I sensed Amber, I couldn't help but think of the ghostly figure's warning. Nightfall. We had until nightfall to seal our bond, or I'd lose everything.

But none of that mattered now. All that mattered was getting to Amber and keeping her safe. Whatever came after, we'd face it together.

CHAPTER 17
AMBER

I stumbled, my foot catching on a tree root. As I hit the ground, I heard Kevin's triumphant yell behind me. This was it. He was going to catch me. And I knew this time, he wouldn't just kidnap me. He would kill me.

Suddenly, a blur of motion crashed into Kevin. Two figures went tumbling back into the forest. Xavier stood, his fist raised, then lowered. The wet thud of him hitting Kevin echoed in the space. Kevin grunted and thrashed, moaning as Xavier hit him again. The sickening sound of breaking bones cracked in the night. I cried out, and Xavier turned to me.

"Do you want me to spare him?"

I remembered what Xavier said about gargoyles being heavier and stronger than humans. I doubted Kevin would survive the fight that had already occurred, anyway. I also knew that if Kevin lived, he would continue to pursue me until one of us was dead. I thought for a moment of the potential mate bond that may have drawn Kevin here, but I couldn't imagine that was true. I knew the kind of man Kevin was and I didn't want to tie him to someone else, not with his control issues. Slowly, I shook my head and turned away.

Kevin's moans turned to a wet gurgle, then silence. I felt nothing, not sadness, not fear, not regret. Not even relief that my ordeal was over. My heart pounded as I waited, frozen in place. After what felt like an eternity, a figure emerged from the trees. It was Xavier, his clothes torn and bloody, but otherwise unharmed.

"He will never bother you again," Xavier said, his voice low and intense.

Finally, a mix of emotions cascaded over me—shock, sadness, but overwhelming relief. Without thinking, I raced towards Xavier and threw my arms around him, not caring about the blood.

Xavier wrapped his arms around me, pulling me close, the strength of his body a solid reassurance that I was safe, protected, and free. Tears broke free, shaking my body in heavy, shuddering sobs, and I clung to Xavier. He rubbed his hands up and down my back in soothing motions until I calmed. I lifted my head and looked at him through watery eyes.

He wiped my eyes with his thumbs. "You're safe now, Amber."

"I can't believe you saved me. You came for me. Thank you."

His expression was uncharacteristically sober as he studied me. "I swore I would always keep you safe as long as you were here. I have kept my word."

I couldn't resist any longer. I pulled his head down to me, capturing his lips with mine, pouring all the love I felt for him into that kiss. Initially, he was unresponsive, stiff and unyielding and I feared I had lost him. Then, his lips softened and opened under mine, and he took over the kiss in an instant, his tongue sweeping into my mouth to tangle with mine. Heat flooded me, replacing the cold terror with arousal and joy at being alive. His hands slid down my back and cupped my butt, lifting me higher against him, until I felt the iron length of his cock pressing against me.

I wrapped my legs around him, rubbing my core against him, my pulse pounding hot and heavy in my veins. He continued to kiss me as if it was our last kiss, and I shifted on his thigh, realizing his leg didn't move with me and it seemed harder than usual.

I broke the kiss, our breathing heavy in the clearing. He studied me with sad eyes. "I'm sorry, Amber. You will be safe now, no matter where you go. Be happy, please."

He dropped his hands but didn't step away. And I realized I was still seated on him, sort of. His thighs formed a seat of a sort, since he was in kind of a crouch. I slid down and realized his legs were stone and the granite was slowly creeping higher up his body.

"What's happening? What's going on?"

Sunlight broke through the forest canopy, shining on his face, and he tilted his head up, closing his eyes for a moment, a look of bliss on his face. "I forgot what sunlight felt like. I only ever felt it as a youngling."

He opened his eyes and faced me, the stone creeping ever higher on his stomach. He gave me a wistful smile. "I would have liked to have spent the rest of our lives together. But I have content knowing you will be safe and happy from now on. Remember me fondly, Amber."

The tightness in my chest intensified as the stone crept ever higher, tendrils streaking his neck and arms. Tears coursed down my cheeks and my throat hurt from crying. I threw my arms around his neck as if I could stop the progression. "You can't turn to stone. Not now. Not when we've found each other."

A realization dawned on me. "Wait! It's daylight. You'll turn back tonight, right? I'll wait for you, right here. I'll be here. Always."

He tried to shake his head, but the stone was overtaking his neck. "No, Amber. I will be stone forever now. This is my curse. I cannot avoid it now. It's over."

His face slowly turned gray and my heart broke. I sobbed, tears falling freely now. I fell to my hands and knees, at an utter loss for how to even go on without Xavier. I had found my courage too late and lost the best man that I could have ever hoped to find. And now I doomed both of us to a cold hell with no rescue.

"I love you, Xavier. Stay with me. Be my mate."

CHAPTER 18
XAVIER

I didn't regret my decision for a moment. While I knew I would be stone forever, stuck in the forest, overgrown by trees and lost to everyone in town and eventually forgotten, I had saved Amber. She would be expelled from Beastly Falls, but her dishonorable male was dead and would never bother her again. She could return to her old life and family and know that she was safe. Maybe she would remember me. Maybe not. It didn't matter. I loved her and was content with my path.

As the stone overtook my body, it felt different. It was no longer a shell, but something deeper. It was my whole body turning stone, something difficult to come back from. I knew this was permanent. I would not be returning at nightfall. As my head began to solidify, I heard words I longed to hear forever.

As if from a distance, I heard crying, words being spoken, but they seemed distant, muffled. As the stone crept higher, dulling my senses, I resigned myself to my fate.

Suddenly, Amber stood before me, her face streaked

with tears. She threw her arms around me, her touch warm against my rapidly cooling skin.

"Xavier, please!" she sobbed, clinging to me desperately. "Stay with me! I accept you, I accept the bond. Please, don't leave me!"

At that moment, realization struck me like lightning. It wasn't Amber who had been rejecting the bond—it was me. I had been so afraid of trapping her, of becoming like those who had cursed our town, that I had closed myself off from the very thing I longed for.

The ghostly figure from before materialized, visible only to me. "Open your heart, Xavier," it whispered.

Taking a deep breath, I finally allowed myself to truly feel - to hope, to love, to trust. I opened myself fully to the bond, and it flooded through me like a tidal wave of warmth and light.

The stone encasing me began to crack and fall away. I felt life surge back into my limbs, my heart beating strong and steady. As the last of the granite crumbled, I wrapped my arms around Amber, pulling her close.

"I'm here," I whispered, my voice hoarse with emotion. "I'm not going anywhere."

I cupped her face in my hands, wiping away her tears with my thumbs. Then, finally, I kissed her. It was a kiss of promise, of new beginnings, of a love strong enough to break curses and transcend time.

As we broke apart, both breathless and laughing through our tears, I knew that whatever challenges lay ahead, we would face them together. The curse was broken, and our future—bright and filled with possibilities— stretched out before us.

EPILOGUE

AMBER

I lay in Xavier's arms, nestled in the cozy bed of his basement lair beneath the library. My fingers traced lazy patterns across his chest as I marveled at the warmth of his skin.

"You feel warmer than before," I murmured, snuggling closer.

Xavier's chest rumbled with a soft chuckle. "That's because I'm not stone anymore," he said, his arms tightening around me.

I tilted my head to look up at him, still in awe of the changes we'd both gone through. "What happens now?" I asked, a mix of excitement and uncertainty in my voice.

Xavier's eyes met mine, filled with love and a newfound peace. "Now, I still protect the library and its knowledge," he explained, "but I'm not a statue unless I choose to be."

The idea of Xavier having that freedom, after centuries of being bound by the curse, made my heart swell with joy.

He held me close, and I sensed he wanted to say something. "What is it, Xavier?"

"Do you regret your choice? You may not leave Beastly Falls, not until the curse falls for everyone, if it ever does. You will lose your family, your friends."

I rolled onto my stomach and proposed my chin on his chest. "Xavier, you're worth it. What I have found with you and Beastly Falls is worth everything outside of here. Besides, I'm convinced that the curse is failing. I think the town wants us to find our mates. I think the town feels as trapped as you all do and is ready to open up again."

Xavier stroked a hand up my back, a small smile playing about his lips. "Maybe you're right, Amber. The town seemed sad, lonely. I hope you're right and the curse breaks soon. Everyone deserves this kind of happiness."

I rested my head on his chest, loving the feel of his heart beating under my cheek. "Now what do we do?"

He stroked my hair, his fingers combing through the long strands. "Now, Amber, we live."

Those simple words held so much promise. We had overcome curses, faced our fears, and found each other against all odds. As I lay there in Xavier's arms, surrounded by the comforting scent of old books and the warmth of our new bond, I felt a sense of belonging I'd never known before.

"We live," I echoed softly, lifting to kiss him.

Whatever challenges the future might hold, whatever adventures awaited us in Beastly Falls, I knew we'd face them together. Our story was just beginning, and I couldn't wait to see where it would lead.

Want more light paranormal romance? Check out Swipe for Orcs, a small town Romeo and Juliet, matchmaker story that vaguely resembles My Big Fat Greek Wedding - With Orcs! Read on for a sample!!

EXCERPT - SWIPE FOR ORCS

DURA

"Y ou have to get mated. You're getting old, Dura."

I winced at the words bellowed at me as I walked in from the kitchen carrying my latest creation, a cheesy stuffed Italian bread recipe. My entire family sat at the rectangular dinner table, staring at me with varying degrees of sadness, disapproval, and, in my younger brother's case, glee that I was on the hot seat and not him for once. I swallowed hard, but regained my composure. Years of hearing versions of the same lecture from my father had given me strategies for dealing with it. It all started with a good meal. My mother always said, the way to an orc's heart is through his stomach. Or through his weaponry, but since a female was never allowed near his weapons, she'd have to settle for a good meal.

I laid the platter with savory bread in front of my father, then quietly stepped to the side and to my seat on the left, across from my younger brother, who smirked.

My father eyed the platter. "What is this?"

"It's something new, Father. An Italian bread stuffed with garlic, cheese, and meat. You pull it apart."

One bushy eyebrow slowly rose as he considered the dish. Orcs had come to the Earthly realm a few generations ago when war had broken out in our home realm. Orcs lived for war. It was our main reason for living. Our entire culture was built around war. Making weapons, training for war, going to war. Despite the capabilities, we had been driven out by political machinations and landed here on Earth. Once we got here, we tried to carry on as we always had—making weapons, training, and looking for how to serve in the wars. Only, humans fought very differently and orcs thought that distance fighting was dishonorable. So, we clung to our old ways, making weapons, training, conducting Orc Games every four years to determine clan status, and slowly were becoming obsolete.

We were forced to live a more civilized life, but there was nothing an orc loved more than a feast with ale, and food we could tear into with our hands. No forks and knives required. Giving my father bread he could tear apart was a small part of home. Maybe it would soften him and make him forget about his absurd statement.

He tore off a piece of the cheesy bread and stuffed it in his mouth, chewing thoughtfully. Then he nodded and slammed a fist on the table. Everyone jumped. "This is good. This is why you'll make an orc a fine mate, though a well-born wife rarely cooks for her husband. She instructs the staff and raises little orclings."

"But I love to bake, Father. I'm good at it," I protested.

My younger brother, Zarod, frantically shook his head and moved his hand across his throat to get me to stop talking. I ignored him. I'd done everything my father had asked. I did the books at the forge. I baked breads and pastry for his business meetings. I hid my work at the local bakery, so no one knew a noble orc's daughter worked for a living.

"By the time your sister Sora was your age, she was married with two orclings and another on the way." Sora beamed at me from across the table, nursing orcling number four. Our father smiled. "A true orc wife. It's time you did your duty."

I could almost feel my freedom slipping away from me. Orc fathers arranged their daughters' marriages. That's how Sora's marriage happened. I had avoided that thus far, playing on my father's affection for me, and my usefulness at the business and my bread. But clearly that favoritism was running out.

"You promised I could pick my own mate."

My father tore off another piece of bread and chewed. "Yes, I gave you until your twenty-fifth birthday, which is in two months. Do I see a potential orc husband on the horizon? No. Have you brought anyone home to meet your family? No. I have to ask myself. Maybe Dura needs help. So your mother and I, we start to ask around the families, gather a list of orcs."

I wanted to sink through the floor. The horror of being talked about at all the orc tables like a commodity, like a piece of meat to be sold at auction, for I had no doubt that he was soliciting offers for my hand in marriage, judging who was giving the most, who was deserving of my hand, depending on their worth to him. I hoped he would take my happiness into consideration, but he mostly considered wealth and status as criteria, whereas I had other standards by which I judged males.

Sora leaned forward. "Father, I'm sure you'll pick a wonderful male, as you did for me."

She gave her husband an adoring look, and I barely suppressed my eye roll. Sora was happy, but she had always wanted to be a wife, unlike me. She was happy popping out orclings. She loved being lady of the manor, running her house like our mother. I thought I might die a slow death if that was my fate.

I had to think fast to counter his plans. "You promised me that I had until my twenty-fifth birthday. You always said an orc was nothing without his word."

My father scowled at me, clearly not liking that I threw his own words back at him. "It's a good thing you're not on the Council or I would have a solid opponent. Fine, you can have until your birthday, in two months, to present to me an orc of good standing as potential husband material. During the Forging Contest at the Orc Games. If you do not, we'll use the contest to find you a mate. Are we clear?"

I sighed. It was the best compromise I was going to get. "Yes, Father. Thank you."

~

A few days later, I found myself sitting in a conference room in the Love Bites Dating Agency, across from a woman in a charcoal gray pinstripe power suit who introduced herself as Beatrix. She was a little weird. Her waist-length gray hair and grayish skin would indicate an older woman, but her skin was flawless and her tone was smooth and sweet, though her white eyes held a sharpness to them that warned me to be on my toes. Another individual joined us, a skinny man, wearing khakis and a t-shirt that said, Beware the Smiling Mage. He wasn't smiling though, not that I could see. His face was buried in his tablet, his long, stringy, dark hair falling around him, and he tapped the screen rapidly.

Beatrix scowled at him, the frown quickly morphing into a smile when she saw me watching.

"Atticus. We have a client," she said, and I could almost hear her teeth grinding.

He waved his hand. "Yes, Dura Ironspike, I'm just tweaking the code. We don't get orcs in the system every day, you know. We have to make adjustments for them."

Beatrix sighed. "Orcs are only just starting to use Love Bites. You generally arrange your marriages but, as you've stayed in this realm and settled around Whynot, we're seeing more and more orcs come to us for matches. It's very exciting."

Atticus grunted. "Exciting isn't quite the word. Challenging is more accurate. You orcs have very specific criteria and it's difficult to find acceptable matches."

I raised my eyebrow. "What does that mean?"

He finally lifted his head and pinned me with hazel eyes, looking a little irritated at my interruption. "Orcs don't consider things like personality and compatibility when finding mates. Instead, they look at clan status, lineage, and connections for bonding. That is not how Love Bites works."

This was precisely why I had tried Love Bites. If I wanted to be sold like a typical orc wife, which was one step up from a broodmare, I would have let my father choose my husband. I knew he would have selected someone kind and considerate, as far as he knew. The orc would have good standing, able to support me financially, and a decent reputation. That didn't always mean he would treat me well behind closed doors, though, with my father as a high councilor, my husband wouldn't dare harm me. But there were many ways to cause harm. Neglect, incompatibility, were just two ways to be unhappy. I wanted a love match, someone to care about me as more than a connection. Someone I could be happy with and love.

I pinned Atticus with a look. "I'm not your typical orc."

He narrowed his gaze. "No, you're not. You're from a prominent family, yet you came here instead of going the traditional route. The question we have is this. Will you accept the match Love Bites provides, knowing it may not fit your family's method of selecting a mate, or will you reject it?"

That was a good question, actually the core question. I would accept an orc that I loved, no matter his status, but would my father? Would my happiness trump his desire for a good match? I wasn't sure I was prepared to see which element my father held as more important—my happiness or my husband's status.

Atticus seemed to sense my hesitation, and he sneered. "This is why we don't like to match orcs."

Beatrix snapped a hand on his arm. "That's enough. If Dura wants to go through the process, we cannot control how she reacts to her match. We have orcs of all statuses in our database."

Atticus opened his mouth as if to protest and Beatrix glared at him until he shut it. I had a bad feeling about the entire process but overruled it. I had no other choice. Dating on my own had been a disaster. I never knew if someone was interested because of my father or me, and if I could trust how they acted. And I was honestly too shy to approach orcs, and most rarely approached me. I really didn't want to be arranged, because I'd seen some of the orcs my father was already considering and they were not my type. He'd been slowly inviting some of them to dinner, and I was unimpressed.

So, Love Bites was my best option.

I straightened in my chair. "I want to move forward. I've completed the questionnaire. What's next?"

Atticus gave a small sigh and scanned the screen. "Everything appears to be in order. All the questions are answered except two. Your favorite breakfast food and a picture?"

I flushed. I was a baker, so what did they think I liked? Pastries and baked goods, of course, as if my picture wouldn't show my slightly rounded figure already. Which brought me to the second area of discomfort. I really didn't want to upload a picture and had hoped to avoid it with the agency.

"I thought Love Bites focused on compatibility. Why do we need a picture?"

Beatrix leaned forward, that polite smile fixed on her face. "There is an element of attraction inherent in all dating profiles. We can easily touch it up a bit, if you prefer."

Atticus snorted. "Everyone does it."

A bright light flashed, and I blinked, momentarily blinded, colored spots dancing in front of me. "What the hell?"

"Simple." He tapped the screen a few times and turned it to show me.

I gasped. My face was smooth, thinner than I expected, and my green skin was a gorgeous shade of emerald that only my sister had ever accomplished with the aid of expensive Nestee Mauder products. I looked almost pretty.

The tablet was whisked out of my hands. "Breakfast food?"

I flushed again and muttered, "Cinnamon rolls."

He nodded, cleaned the screen with a wet wipe, then handed me the tablet. "Lick."

I frowned. "Excuse me?"

"Lick the screen right in the center. Last step."

I wrinkled my nose but did it. An orange taste exploded on my tongue. "Orange?"

He took it back with a disgusted sound. "It's not a test. We know it's orange. We don't know why, okay?"

He shoved back from the conference room table and stalked from the room. Beatrix pasted her polite smile on her face. "Here are instructions to download our app to your phone. You'll be able to log in and review your matches there, though, for the first time, we ask that you come and review them with us so we can ensure there are no tweaks to your profile to be made. Then you can arrange your dates via the app. Don't make any contact outside the app until you've had your date."

She stood. "And please keep us posted. We'll be in touch in the next couple of days when the profile is complete and your first set of matches are ready."

I stood, taking the pamphlet with log in instructions. "Everything is private, right?"

"Of course. No one can interfere with our algorithms."

I followed her outside. "Do you have a lot of orcs on the app?"

Beatrix continued to give that smile that was really irritating me. "Of course, dear. We pride ourselves on our success rate."

That wasn't quite an answer, but time was ticking and I needed an acceptable mate soon. I hoped Love Bites would come through.

~

Want to read more? Click here for Swipe for Orcs, a small town Romeo and Juliet, matchmaker story that vaguely resembles My Big Fat Greek Wedding - With Orcs!

Also by Sabrina Silvers

THE DIRIGO PACK SERIES

The Dirigo Pack. One of the prominent wolf shifter packs in the United States. Led by Duncan MacKinnon and his family of three sons and a daughter, they're dedicated to protecting their family, their pack, and living a life of honor. But they face their greatest adversary when Kayleigh MacKinnon is kidnapped by an unknown enemy and they face treachery among other packs. Only through love and the strongest of will can they survive.

Forbidden Moon (Prequel) Can a mating bond bridge the gap between feuding packs ... or will it destroy them all?

Maya Wessex and Garrett Colvin were childhood friends until their pack rivalry tore then apart. When they meet again as adults, the mating bond roars to life, giving them a second chance at life, love, and mating.

Alpha's Moon (Book 1) The Alpha-Heir and a hybrid shifter-witch unite to find the Pack Princess when she's kidnapped by an old enemy. They must fight their mating urges and challenges from within the pack and the enemies outside to find their love and save his sister.

Moon Madness (Book 2) A wolf who almost lost control of his beast must dive into the belly of shifter politics with a tough female enforcer as a body guard to protect his pack and save his sister. While navigating politics, they must overcome their own prejudices and attraction, while fighting the knives aimed at their back to save their pack.

Feral Moon (Book 3) An Alpha slowly losing his mind to moon madness and a lack of mate is given a mate through treachery and deceit, only to find the kidnapped princess of his rival is the mate who can save him. Will he keep her and risk war or will he let her go and lose himself to the madness that will destroy him and his pack, and possibly all of the shifter world?

Rejected Moon (Book 4) As Nik and Isa confront the mating bond that ties them together, can they navigate the dangers of their present, and overcome the pain of their past to find a new future, healed and whole together? Or will they fall back into despair, alone and broken? Rejected.

∼

Orc World Series

Rescued By Her Monster Mercenaries (Villains Do It Better series)

Trapped in a realm straight out of a fantasy novel? Check. Sold off as a mate in a bizarre auction? Double check. And guess what? The bidders aren't charming princes but rather orcs, minotaurs, and other creatures straight out of my worst nightmares.

As if my love life wasn't complicated enough, we've got malevolent forces lurking around, threatening to ruin our newfound romance. But hey, at least I've got two strapping warriors by my side. Who needs a knight in shining armor when you've got an orc and a minotaur?

Now, the big question looms: Do I try to find my way back home or do I stay in this fantastical world with my unlikely mates? Love, danger, and some seriously weird creatures await.

Collected by the Orc (Orcs Unbound)

After my boss makes a pass at me during an outdoor

leadership retreat, I somehow get lost in the Colorado woods and end up in a weird fantasy world right out of Lord of the Rings, complete with orcs! Only this orc is sexy and protective, saying he'll help me get home.

As we journey through his world and he shows a softer side, not to mention a smokin' hot sexy side, I begin to wonder if it would be that bad to stay here.

But I sense he's keeping secrets and, when a dethroned orc prince and his band of merry rebels show up to kill my escort for crimes against the people, should I defend my protector or run screaming into the night?

ALSO BY SABRINA AND ZOEY - WHYNOT!

Looking for something lighter? Check out the books in the Love Bites series!

Welcome to the town of Whynot where love is just a Swipe Right away!

Located along the River Sticks, the town caters to a diverse population of magical species due to the abundance of natural resources, temperate weather, and ease of Interstate access.

Love Bites, the most popular matchmatching agency in the tri-state area, offers in-person matching or cutting edge technology in the form of a dating app. Just upload a picture, fill out a questionnaire and lick the screen to connect with your best matches. The technomages are aware the app tastes like oranges. They're working on it.

One Click this collection paranormal romcom stories about witches, banshees, strigoi, and wendigos searching for their fated matches one date at a time. After all, with unreliable dating magic involved, three old crones running the office who may or may not be the Three Fates, and what could possibly go wrong?

Welcome to Whynot - Swipe for Rivals

A forbidden love between a light elf who must marry to take on the ruling mantle of his family and a dark elf, desperate to ally her family with another, threatens to ignite a war that could destroy them all. When a matchmaking witch and a meddlesome cousin interfere in the dating agency's algorithm to pair the enemies, tensions flare, but love also blooms. Can the lovers use their love to bridge the family feud and thwart a war between their people?

Available now!

Swipe for Orcs

Two orcs... One an outcast, one avoiding an arranged marriage. Both come to Love Bites hoping to find their perfect match. When they find each other, all seems perfect, until their romance is threatened by her father's disapproval of his lower status. Determined to win her heart, he enters a prestigious contest with her hand in marriage as the prize. It won't be easy though - with witches and orcs interfering at every turn, he'll have to pull out all the stops to prove himself and win her hand in marriage.

Available now!

Swipe for Ghosts

Love is just a swipe away - if you're not afraid to walk the plank.

Edge, once a fledgling pirate sailing alongside Blackbeard, is now spiritually bound to a plank of wood from the gallows where he met his tragic end. Haunted by his past and seeking redemption, he never expected to find love in such an unusual way. Immy, a young witch from a powerful family, desires a quiet, peaceful life. Lacking confidence in her own powers, she's determined to find love and prove to herself that she can forge her own path.

Together, Edge and Immy embark on a heartwarming adventure filled with magical mishaps, ghostly capers, and the undeniable power of love. As they navigate life after their paranormal dating app fiasco, they'll learn that sometimes the most unexpected encounters can create the most enchanting stories.

In Swipe for Ghosts, love transcends the barriers of time and the supernatural, proving that even the most unlikely pairings can lead to a happily ever after. This delightful tale of romance, self-discovery, and adventure will sweep you off your feet and leave you rooting for the extraordinary couple that fate brought together.

Available 2024

About Sabrina Silvers

Sabrina Silvers began her writing career dreaming of elves, orcs, and hobbits in the fantasy section of her local library, looking in wardrobes for Narnia and Aslan, and hunting for gnomes in the forest. To her dismay, she never found any of them except between the pages of her books. So, she had to go out and create them for herself, leading to her lifelong love of reading and writing and dreaming about adventures, fantasy creatures and love in fantasy lands! She divides her time between writing sexy contemporary romances under a different pen name, reading, knitting and being owned by a very spoiled cocker spaniel who does not share her love of fantasy creatures.

For upcoming releases and other information including access to bonus content, sign up for her newsletter at her website at: https://www.sabrinasilvers.com

- facebook.com/SabrinaSilversAuthor
- instagram.com/sabrinasilversauthor
- tiktok.com/@sabrinasilversauthor
- amazon.com/stores/Sabrina-Silvers/author/B08XGWXHF8
- bookbub.com/authors/sabrina-silvers
- goodreads.com/sabrina_silversauthor